World Unraveled

Book One of The Scorched Earth Saga

by Anthoney Pavelich

This first book is dedicated to everyone afraid to follow their dreams. I have a patch on my riding vest that says, "Pain Is Temporary, Regret Is Forever". Don't live with regret, chase your dreams.

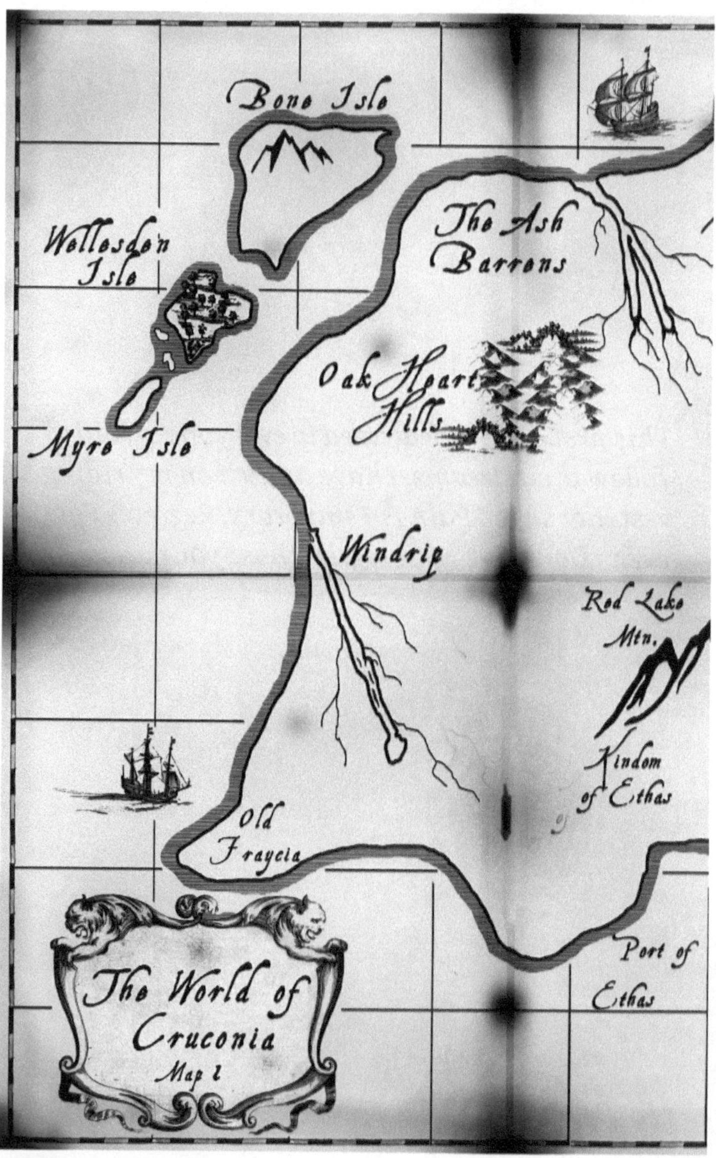
Bone Isle
Wellesdon Isle
The Ash Barrens
Oak Heart Hills
Myre Isle
Windrip
Red Lake Mtn.
Kindom of Ethas
Old Fraycia
Port of Ethas
The World of Cruconia
Map 1

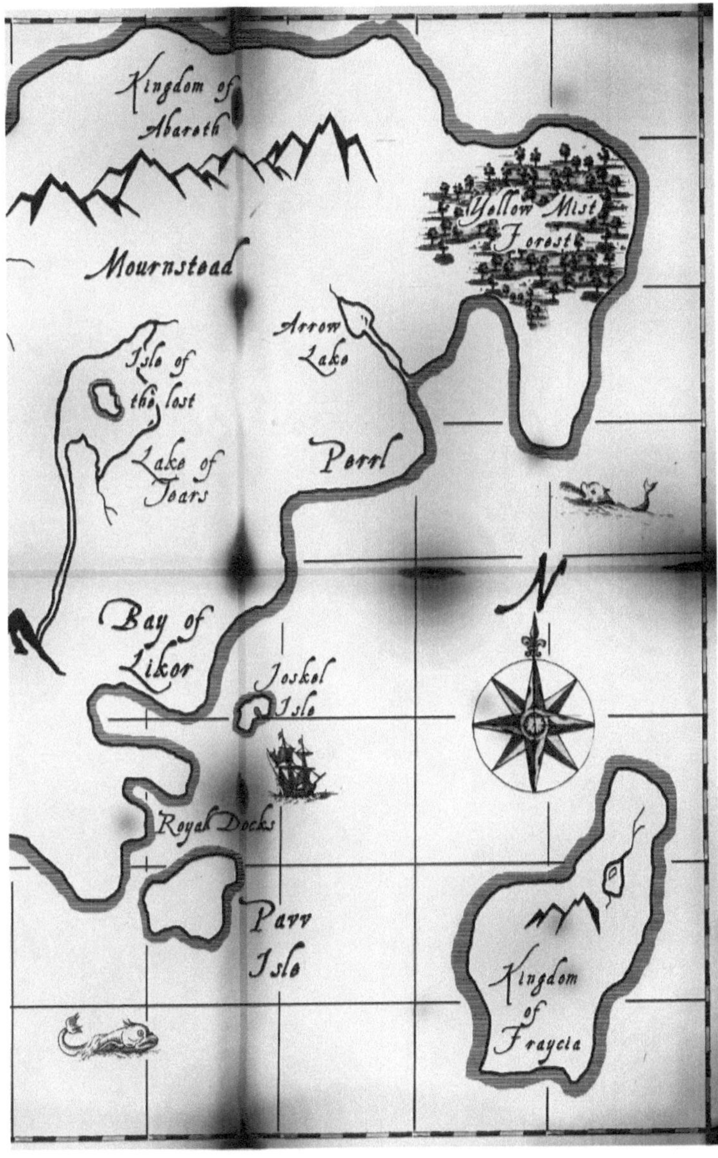

Kingdom of Abareth
Mournstead
Yellow Mist Forest
Isle of the lost
Arrow Lake
Lake of Tears
Perrl
Bay of Likor
Joskol Isle
Royal Docks
Pavr Isle
Kingdom of Fraycia
N

Acknowledgements

For many years I dreamt of writing a story. One that I could enjoy, but one to bring joy to others. After many tries and pauses, this story come to fruition. The story of a young man exploring love, magic and things he could only imagine existed.

I need to make sure I thank a long-time friend, Vincent. Without him, you would not have a visual of what the world of Cruconia looks like in this first book. It gets bigger.

Bringing Gevan to life was a bit of internal struggle due the fact that he is gay. There is the possibility this will not be widely accepted by fans of the genre, but it is the truth about who I am and what I wanted to write. This isn't a story about the character being gay, it's a story about his journey in life.

This would not have been possible without the love and support of my husband, Matthew. He supported my desire to take this journey. I am lucky every day to have him in my life and on my side. I love you, Matthew.

Chapter 1

Gevan shot up in bed, heart racing and temporarily confused where he was. This wasn't the first time he had heard this voice in his dreams. But this time was different; the message had an urgency to it.

Gevan was sweating and his nightshirt was drenched. He climbed out of bed and lifted his nightshirt off. Walking over to the single window in his attic room, he caught his reflection in the window before opening it. He was a handsome man by most standards, in his eighteenth year, with dark red hair that was thick on his head, chest, and legs. He was of average height, just under six feet tall.

The window was on a hinge and opened outward. Gevan placed a long wooden stick in the frame to hold it open. He stood naked in the moonlight shining through the window. As it reflected in his green eyes, he tried to recall the dream he just had beyond the words he remembered. There was nothing else he could recall, just the words that gave him chills.

Gevan had shared a room with his sister downstairs for years, and hadn't moved into the attic until they were both in their early teens. Their mother had felt it was best to give them both privacy since they were getting older. He was glad to have his privacy, and he liked the window; but when the dreams had started over a year ago, he longed to wake up to someone he could talk to.

The dreams always faded within minutes, just leaving an echo of a feeling. The feeling was similar to dread, but he couldn't put a name to it. He tried to talk to his mother about them once; she told him his imagination was fuelled by his late-night snacking habits.

His room was simple, with just a bed, a dresser, a desk and chair, and a sink. Gevan turned from the window and walked around the bed on his right to the dresser on the opposite side. Opening a drawer, he pulled out a clean nightshirt. Slipping it over his toned body, he walked back to the window and stared up at the palace it overlooked: the royal palace of Ethas.

Ethas was the largest of the three known kingdoms on the world of Cruconia. It was also the most modern, thanks to being at the base of the largest mountain in the land. The positioning and slope of the city allowed them to have running water, which the other two kingdoms didn't have.

It wasn't possible to see the top of the

mountain from the village; it seemed to rise endlessly upward, disappearing into the clouds. Gevan frequently found himself thinking about the top of that mountain, wondering what it looked like... wondering if he might go there someday. There, and other places.

Gevan and his family lived a short ride from the eastern palace gates, where all the suppliers of goods and services entered. His mother owned a bakery that supplied bread and sweets to the king, his family, and guests. Gevan and his sister, Lily, had been helping their mother in the bakery since they could stand on a stool and knead bread.

The dream was beginning to fade. He could remember a rumbling of rocks, shadows moving quickly, and the sense of urgency. Even those memories would be gone soon.

Gevan went back to his rough bed, nothing more than a wooden frame, planks of wood, and a mattress filled with hay and a layer of feathers he had been gathering around the pond near the palace gate.

As he lay back down, his mind wandered back to thoughts of travelling and adventures. He had grown up wanting to travel, but he was destined to take over the business with his sister.

Gevan let out a big sigh, closed his eyes, and drifted back to sleep.

∞ ∞ ∞

Lily had been up since before dawn with her mother preparing the day's pastry and bread order for the palace. As she finished packing the bags with loaves of bread and baskets with muffins and other pastries, Gevan came down the ladder from his attic bedroom. The ladder fit flush against the furthest corner of the kitchen. It went halfway up the door of his room, so he could easily open and close it from the ladder. The ovens in the kitchen underneath, and fireplaces in the other rooms below his room, helped heat the attic in the colder seasons without needing a fireplace.

The other ovens and fireplace in the kitchen also heated the water tank in the other part of the attic, which was used for washing and showers. The tank was filled from the kingdom's intricately designed and constructed water supply, which was fed from a lake on top of the mountain.

The last king of Ethas had created the system after the end of the last great war, around 100 years ago. It was the water system that had boosted the village population, and eventually made Ethas the wealthiest of the three kingdoms.

"About time you got out of bed," announced Lily, loudly enough that the palace guards a block away could have heard. "We've been up for hours preparing the delivery and it's almost ready, no thanks to you!"

Gevan looked at his sister through blurred eyes. Just under two years older, she stood less than a few inches shorter than him. But instead of dark red hair, hers was pitch-black like their mother's. He always thought his sister was beautiful – which was why he was always so protective of her. He didn't want the village boys to get any ideas.

Since their father wasn't around, Gevan felt it was his duty to make sure Lily was safe. He wanted to make sure any man settled on marrying his sister was worth it and not just out for fun. Lily would often get frustrated at her brother's over-protectiveness, but she also appreciated the times he was able to fend off those unwanted advances.

"Gevan," Lily said in a stern voice. "Are you listening to me?"

"What? I will be ready soon!" Gevan grumbled through his sleepiness. "I will get the horse hitched to the cart and get it loaded." Gevan always took the morning delivery to the palace kitchen. It was his first stop on his daily deliveries before dropping off baked goods at some of the local inns and markets. The Twisted Feather Bakery was not the only bakery in the village, but it was the largest.

"I asked if you were going to be home for dinner."

"Sorry, Lily, I will be home. I have plans

later with some friends after."

"Then you two need to get a move on if all this work is going to be done before it's time for breakfast again," piped up their mother Vita, who had been silently recounting the order as she listened to her children's banter. "There's a lot to get done before dinner, so get a move on."

Vita Demeter turned around with the warm, open smile for which she was well-known. She was grateful how close her two children were, considering they didn't have the same father; even more grateful that they didn't know it.

Vita had opened the bakery after arriving in the village when was Lily was only two months old. Lily's father had died of an illness while Vita was still pregnant with her. She had no family, and his family hadn't approved of the marriage, so she had ended up in Ethas.

She had money saved, and with the sale of the home she had with her late husband, she had enough – barely – to buy this building and start the bakery.

Lily had been only eight months old when Vita met Gevan's father. He was a tall man, just over six feet. Dark features, but the reddest hair. And his eyes were as green as the grass. He just showed up one day, asking directions. He looked as if he had been travelling a long time. Vita gave him a muffin and directions to the southern gate of the palace.

He returned the next morning, and after

that they were inseparable. At least until he came to her one day three months later to say he had to leave. It broke her heart. It would be years later before she understood why, and he learned he had a son.

∞∞∞

Gevan was pulling up to the palace gate with the morning delivery when he noticed that something was different. There was much more activity than usual. Instead of the usual one guard, there were three. None of them were familiar to him. He heard yelling, hammering, and what sounded like metal on metal.

"Morning, sirs." Gevan was always respectful to the guards. He started to ride through the gate as he did every morning, but suddenly the closest guard stepped in the path of his horse and cart, causing the horse to get nervous and begin to turn off the path to the right. Gevan pulled the reins tight and put the horse back on the path.

"What's your business, boy?" The guard looked to be a middle-aged man, silver hair, about a foot taller than Gevan. He was the tallest guard Gevan had ever seen.

Gevan paused in shock. He had never been stopped before. But just as he was about to answer, a familiar face came around from the other side of the gate, "He's all right, this is the daily delivery to the kitchen from the bakery." A younger short blond-haired, but still middle-aged soldier smiled at Gevan.

"Good morning, Lieutenant Smark! What's with all the guards?" Gevan asked, unable to restrain his curiosity.

"It's Captain Smark now, Gevan. We are just having some new recruits and training exercises. Nothing to worry about." Gevan had known Smark since he was a kid; the guard speaking more formally than usual with him gave Gevan a sense something more was behind all the new recruits.

Gevan looked at the four men and replied, "Well congratulations, Captain!"

"Be on your way to the kitchen and steer clear of the exercise, don't want to spook that horse of yours again." Captain Smark gave Gevan a smile without the other guards seeing it, helping Gevan relax a bit after how he had been greeted at first.

"Yes, sir. Have a good day," was all Gevan could say as he guided his cart through the gate. His curiosity was high, but he knew better than to push the newly promoted captain. Though they knew each other well, Smark had made it clear that now was not the time to show their familiarity in front of the other three guards.

As he entered the gate, Gevan was surprised at the bustling activity all around him. So surprised that he almost steered his horse and cart into an oncoming man carrying two empty bushels.

"Gevan! Watch where you're going!" yelled the man. "An unusual sight, isn't it?" Gevan looked over and saw Brody, a man he'd only met a few times through his friend Jack. He usually made his delivery in the afternoons.

"Brody, what's going on here?"

"I'm not completely sure. The kitchen girl, what's her name again, Shelly? Cheryl?"

Gevan grimaced. "It's Marla. No wonder you've never dated anyone. You're so bad and remembering their names!" They both chuckled. "Now, what did MARLA say?" Gevan continued.

"You've not been seen around with anybody I know of either," countered Brody. "I've had my eyes on a few ladies, but still holding out for the king's daughter. Anyway. *Marla* couldn't give any gossip. They all woke up early this morning to the sounds of all these men putting on armor and getting swords ready for practice. Everyone is saying it's just routine."

This was no routine Gevan had ever known in the eighteen years he'd lived in the village. There were at least two hundred men in the palace yard. They all were in groups of four, inspecting each other's armor for fit and ensuring the correct form. All their helms were held in one hand, while their swords were all sheathed on the opposite side.

"We shouldn't stand here and watch,"

Gevan said after a moment. "I need to get the delivery to the kitchen. Why only two bushels today? The orchard should be full of fruit right now."

Brody's family owned an orchard with fruit trees about an hour's ride outside the outer boundaries of the village. It had been there for generations, from what Gevan knew. Brody was four years older than Gevan and was the only child. He stood a few inches taller and was darker than Gevan, both skin and hair. He was growing a close beard but was of average build.

"Shorty asked me to come back for the cart after lunch to unload it. They are busy making lunch for all these men." Brody took a leftover apple out of one of the bushels and took a bite.

"I'm taking these to town for some supplies, and I'm stopping off at your bakery for some of your mother's sweet rolls."

"Well, get going if you want any," Gevan replied. "They sell quick. I'd better get to the kitchen." They said their goodbyes and Gevan rode to the kitchen delivery door. It was only five minutes from the gate, but all the activity had him riding slower as he wondered about everything going on around him.

Gevan pulled his cart up to the kitchen delivery door as the kitchen lead cook came out to meet him. He was a stout man, only about five feet tall, and in his late fifties. He was wearing a dingy white smock over his grey wool trousers. His boots were ankle-high and he was almost as wide as he was tall. But he carried himself with pride and a sense of authority.

"Good to finally see you Gevan, we have a lot of mouths to feed today!"

"Hi Shorty, sorry I am a bit behind. All this commotion took me by surprise." Shorty was the cook's nickname; as a kid he had been called Shorty Korty. His name was Kurt, but he had decided long ago that it was better to own the nickname than be bullied.

"Yeah, yeah. I don't have time to worry about what this *routine exercise* is, I just know I have two hundred extra mouths to feed. Speaking of which, can you deliver an extra fifty loaves of bread tomorrow?" Shorty's question was directed to Gevan, but his eyes were on the commotion of the soldiers in the yard.

"I will stop back home on my way to make the other deliveries and let my mother know." Gevan knew this meant a bit of extra work for him tonight, likely a working dinner. But it also meant more money for the family.

"How is Vita?" Shorty asked. "I haven't seen her in ages, not since you started making the deliveries."

"Mother's doing well. We have had a good growth in the business. She is thinking of hiring an extra pair of hands soon. I'll see you tomorrow morning!" Gevan had heard the stories of Shorty making eyes at his mother, so the less information the better.

"Good day, Gevan! My best to your mom!" Shorty smirked as he turned and ordered two young boys to unload the cart as he returned to the kitchen.

Gevan began the trip home, which was only about 20 minutes from the kitchen. He was still curiously watching every move of the guards as he headed to the gate. There was something that didn't feel "routine" about this, besides the fact he had never seen this many guards. He had no name for the feeling. He had felt this sense of disquiet only a few times. Usually right after his night-mares.

∞∞∞

When Gevan arrived home, Brody had al-ready arrived, and was talking to Lily in the corner of the kitchen. She seemed to be blushing, and he was smiling.

"Brody, don't you have other stops to make?" Gevan snapped. He wasn't too sure about them flirting; he felt Brody was too much of a womanizer to be with *his* sister.

"Leave him alone!" snapped his mother. Vita wanted her daughter to find a husband, and she liked Brody. They had a good business rela-tionship with the family, and it seemed Brody was now taking over a lot of duties as he become a young man.

"It's ok, ma'am," Brody said with a smirk. "He's right, I have to pick up some supplies and then head back to the royal kitchen for my cart before long."

"Speaking of the royal kitchen, Shorty asked for an extra 50 loaves of bread for tomorrow's delivery, "Gevan said. "I am guessing he will need extra for a while." Gevan didn't send Shorty's regards to his mother.

"Well, it looks like it's going be a long night!" Vita said with a frustrated sigh. "Lily, is your friend Minna free to help, do you think?" Minna had been learning the trade under Vita and Lily for the last few months. She went to school with Lily and was living with her grandparents since her parents had passed.

"I will go over and ask, I am sure she is." Lily knew Minna would be; her grandfather was a blacksmith and her grandmother just took care of the family. Minna didn't know what trade to get into since her parents had been fishers and after their accident, she was afraid of getting on a boat.

Vita's calculating gaze fell upon Gevan. "If you're going to meet your friends and get up early to load all this bread, you'd better get going yourself!"

"Yes, Mother!" Gevan, replied, grinning. He started to leave, but then turned to Brody. "You coming?"

Brody turned and smiled at Lily as the two men left. Lily was right behind them on her way to go talk to Minna.

Chapter 2

Minna stayed to eat dinner with the Demeter family, since she was working to get the large order for the next day.

As Gevan helped clear the table after dinner, he asked his mother, "How much more do you need to get done for tomorrow?"

"We have about 20 more loaves to bake, so we should be ready in a few hours," she responded as she poured herself a cup of coffee. Gevan looked at his mother as she leaned against the sink sipping the coffee and seemingly staring into nothing. He knew she enjoyed the work she did, but he felt sometimes she looked like she was missing something.

"Do you have all the supplies you need?" His mother didn't seem to react. Gevan knew they were well stocked, but he wanted to sound like he was willing to run some errands before he met his friends for the night.

"Stop avoiding the question, Gevan, and just ask Mother if you are needed any more tonight!" Lily was always good at reading her brother's intentions.

Gevan shot a glare towards Lily and then looked over at Minna, who was at the sink, smirking. "Do you need an escort home or are you staying a while yet?"

"I am going to be here a while," the girl replied and seemed to blush, her pale skin turning flush with red and not looking directly at Gevan. She quickly turned toward the sink and continued cleaning dishes. "Your mother offered me to stay the night here. I will be staying in Lily's room with her. Thank you, though."

Gevan dismissed the girl's reaction and looked at Vita. "Mother, if you don't need me, I am going to shower and get ready for the evening." Gevan had plenty of time before he was to meet his friends, so he knew he had time to rest a bit.

"No, we are good here, Son," she said, as if coming out of her distracted trance. "Just please make sure you are in shape to get up early. We have a lot more than normal to load for tomorrow. I made a few extra sweet rolls and cookies for the palace." Vita wanted to send some extra for the kitchen staff working overtime.

"Of course, Mother," Gevan said with a wink and chuckle as he turned and went up to his room. The three women began to finish up the dishes and prepare the other 20 loaves for the next day.

Upstairs in his room, Gevan opened the window and stared at the palace and the gate he had ridden through earlier in the day. He still had a feeling something wasn't right; he just was not sure how to explain it.

He turned away from the window and removed his boots, trousers, and shirt. Laying down on his bed, he listened to the familiar, comforting sounds of the women talking and baking downstairs, and let his mind drift to what he had seen in the palace yard that day. Where did all the men come from? How did they get to the palace without anyone in the village seeing them? Before he knew it, Gevan had dozed off.

*I have protected and helped others before you.
You can trust me when we meet. I have been
at rest until now, waiting for you.*

Gevan jolted awake. That voice again in his dreams. He had that same feeling of dread again. But this time it also gave him a sense of comfort.

Laying there, he listened and heard the three women in the kitchen downstairs, still working. The fragrance of the baking bread permeated his attic room. He stood up and walked over the window and looked at the moon. The sky was clear, and the stars shone bright. From the look, he hadn't slept more than half an hour.

Gevan walked over the water basin and

turned the spout to put water into the tan porcelain bowl. He took a towel out of a drawer in the sink stand and began to wash up. He didn't want to go back downstairs to shower. He finished washing up and put on some clean clothes and headed down the ladder to the kitchen.

"Where are you all meeting up tonight, Gevan?" asked Lily.

"Why, Sister? Are you planning on crashing my fun night?" Gevan was just poking fun, but Lily didn't seem to find it funny, considering the look she flashed him. "Whoa," he continued, chuckling as he held his hands up for mock protection. "Don't burn a hole in me with those eyes! We are meeting at the Red Lake Tavern. You're so serious!"

"Well, have a good time, and don't worry about us here still slaving away," Lily shot back. This made both Vita and Minna laugh.

Shaking his head, Gevan turned and walked out the door, shouting, "Good night, don't burn down the house while I'm out!"

The Red Lake Tavern was about half an hour's walk toward the lakeshore. It was named after the lake that supplied all the water to the palace and village from the top of the mountain. Although it had never been seen by anyone in the village, it was rumoured that the water was blood-red, and it was clear only due to being filtered by the mountain it flowed through.

There were many stories about what caused

the water to be red, ranging from the dirt being red to the lake bed being layered with rubies. Since nobody in living memory had ever actually seen the lake, there was no actual proof that the water was even really red.

As Gevan walked, he was lost in thought about his earlier dream. The change in how it made him feel, the new and different message... it all seemed to progress toward something. His mother told him these were just dreams appearing into his thoughts later, after he awoke... but were they?

He pushed it from his mind and started looking at the buildings he was walking past. This close to town, most of them were closed shops with living space on the upper floors. Light streamed out from the windows, and laughter echoed in the streets below. At this time of the evening, most families were talking about their day and getting ready for tomorrow. It seemed so normal, considering what Gevan had witnessed that morning. It was like the village was unaware of all the additional soldiers in the yard that day.

"Excuse me, do you know where the constable's office is?" asked a gruff voice from the alley on his right as he was walking past. Gevan was in such deep thought that he jumped. "Sorry," the stranger said, "I didn't mean to startle you."

"No problem, I was... thinking of something," Gevan responded. He looked guardedly at the dark alley as a short man who looked to be in his later years stepped out of the darkness into the light of the streetlamp. "The office is two blocks up the street towards the palace." Gevan pointed out the direction.

"Thank you," replied the stranger. "Have a pleasant evening with your friends at the Red Lake."

As Gevan looked at the strange man and thanked him, the man nodded and walked in the direction opposite from where he had said he wanted to go.

Gevan took two steps and then turned suddenly to call out to the man. How did he know where Gevan was going?

The man wasn't there.

A chill ran up Gevan's spine. He stood there for what seemed like five minutes, trying to remember what the man looked like, but he just couldn't recall. All he could remember was that the man was about a foot shorter than him.

Gevan turned and started walking toward the tavern. He glanced back again, but all he saw were two women walking on the opposite side of the street. They were carrying some baskets of what looked like cloth. There was still no man.

After another ten minutes he arrived at the Red Lake Tavern. The tavern was run by the same family that ran the boarding house next door, Red Lake House, but although they were attached, there was no public door between the two. This was to keep the tavern patrons and tenants of the boarding house separate.

Gevan pulled open the front door of the tavern and walked in to a noisy and smoky room. The door opened up just before the bar, which was tended by a short middle-aged man. He was balding, with just crest of dark hair around his head and a few longer hairs combed over the top. It wasn't a successful attempt to hide his baldness. Two women and one man seemed to be the only people working as servers tonight, all for a room of forty to fifty patrons.

Gevan looked around the room for his friends. Centered on the far wall was a large fireplace, but considering it was the middle of the summer, there wasn't a fire in it at the moment. To the right were all the tables, filled with mostly men. Most tables were built to seat four, but some were pulled together, as was the case in the far corner. That was where he saw his friend Jack with Brody and three other men.

Gevan gave a wave to Jack as he made his way through the maze of tables to the corner.

"Gevan! It's been too long," Jack yelled as Gevan approached the group.

"Welcome back, Jack," Gevan replied as he gave his best friend a hug. Jack was a few inches taller than Gevan, but only a month older. He had blond hair and blue eyes and was clean shaven like his father. His hair was short, almost like a soldier would keep it.

Jack had been on a trip with his mother to

see his aunt and cousins. His uncle had been sick, and they went to help out with the store while he recovered.

"How is your uncle?" Gevan asked as he reached the table.

"He's fully recovered, thank you. Let me introduce to the crowd. You know Brody." Brody was sitting across the table from Jack.

"Yes," Gevan said with squinted eyes, and smirked as he continued, "just saw him today, too many times." Brody laughed.

"These other two brothers next to him are John and Fredrick, they are friends of my cousins." Gevan shook both their hands across the table as they exchanged greetings. They looked very alike, though John was older. Both had dark hair, green eyes, and full beards which were well-groomed.

"And finally, this is Harry." Jack motioned to the man sitting directly in front of Gevan. Harry's back had been to him as he was introduced to the others. Harry stood up and turned to face Gevan.

"It's a pleasure to meet you, Gevan." Harry was equal in height to Gevan. His hair was not too long, just covering his ears and a dark blond, while his eyes were dark brown. He had a slight beard of the same colour, which was purposefully groomed close. He smiled as he took Gevan's hand to shake it.

Gevan just stared at Harry; there was something about him. As he shook his hand, he looked into Harry's eyes. Though dark, they seem to shine.

After what seemed like minutes, Gevan realized he hadn't said anything, just stood there shaking Harry's hand. Finally, he replied, "Likewise." It was all he could get out.

"Sit down, Gevan," Jack said, not noticing. "I'll order us another round. The service is a bit slow, two of the waitresses didn't show tonight. The bartender has his nephew helping out." With that, Jack waived down one of the women and ordered a round of ale for the table and a shot of whiskey for everyone.

Harry moved over a seat so that Gevan was between him and Jack, with Brody and the brothers across from them.

"How long are you two here for?" Gevan asked the brothers.

Frederick waved a dismissive hand. "We leave day after tomorrow. We're taking a skiff from the docks to Joskel Island. Our family has a house there." Joskel Island was a little island a day's sail off the coast where prominent families had vacation homes. It wasn't large, but the homes were handed down from generation to generation.

"We are going to do some repairs, our parents will be joining us in two weeks for the rest of the summer," added John.

Gevan had been trying to get the nerve to ask Harry anything to get to know more, but Jack beat him to it. "Harry, tell us about you."

"How do you know this scamp next to me?" Gevan asked, jerking a thumb at Jack.

"I don't, not really," Harry replied with a smile. "I just met the group about half hour before you joined us. I was sitting alone at the table next to theirs and they needed more seats for when you arrived. So, they asked me to join, out of necessity I guess." The last part Harry said in jest.

"And I am glad we did," Jack replied as the waitress brought their drinks. Jack raised his shot glass to toast the group. "To necessity!"

"To necessity!" everyone chimed in and downed their whiskey.

The rest of the evening was uneventful. The brothers spoke of their house and the lands they owned, which were many. Brody occasionally mentioned Lily, which got under Devan's skin. Brody really seemed to like her; gods forbid he thought Lily liked him.

Jack did a lot of talking about his uncle and the store they were running while they were gone, but nothing about the soldiers who were in the palace. Maybe his father hadn't told him, or he wasn't allowed to say.

Harry was quieter, laughing at some jokes and looking at Gevan a lot. He was staying at the boarding house next door after arriving on the boat today. He hadn't divulged where he came from or how long he was staying.

After hours had gone by, many ales and too many stories, it was time for Gevan to head out.

He had an early morning. "Well boys, I have to get home. We have a large delivery for the palace tomorrow."

"I'll walk you out; it's been a long day and I need some rest." Harry stood up and shook the two brothers' hands and Brody's. He looked at Jack. "Thank you for commandeering my table tonight. I had a good time. I'm sure I will see you around."

"My pleasure!" Jack replied, then gave his best friend a hug. "It was good to see you, Gevan. We need to catch up soon."

In a low voice Gevan replied, "Yes. I am very interested in hearing what you know about those 'routine practices' going on in the palace."

Jack stepped back with a forced smile and his hands still on Gevan's shoulders. "We will talk soon. Have a good night," and with a wink he added, "behave." Gevan blushed.

Harry followed Gevan out of the tavern. Once on the street outside, Gevan turned to say goodnight to Harry and found him standing there under the light of the streetlamp just looking at him.

"Again, it was nice to meet you tonight, Gevan." Harry was polite and yet reserved. He took Gevan's hand to shake it, but there was something different about his handshake.

"You too, Harry. You didn't say how long you are staying."

"I have no immediate plans to leave. Can we

meet up again tomorrow? I feel we should get to know each other better."

"Yes," was all Gevan could manage to get out. He found himself oddly speechless in front of Harry. "My mother runs the Twisted Feather Bakery at the top of this street. I have deliveries til midday."

"I'm staying here, as you know. If you're in the area tomorrow, stop in and ask for me. If not, I may need some home-baked goods later in the day." Harry smiled and walked next door to the boarding house. Before he walked in, he turned one more time and nodded at Gevan.

Gevan nodded back and turned to walk back up toward home. It had to be sometime after midnight; he had lost track of time. All the way home he recalled Harry's eyes and how they shone even though they were so dark.

Then he remembered the look on Jack's face when he said they would talk, referring to the extra soldiers. Something didn't fit. He would have to make sure to get with Jack at some point tomorrow.

Chapter 3

"Did you hear me, Lewis?" Strand asked the king.

Strand had been a family advisor and friend to the royal family of Ethas for a few generations, beginning with Lewis's grandfather. He was a short, stout man. His hair was white, almost pure white, on his head and his beard. He wore his hair short, and it didn't look as if he took time to do anything to make it look presentable. His beard almost reached the belt that tied the simple brown robe he wore.

"Yes, Strand. I heard you," King Lewis said in a distracted tone as he turned to face Strand. "Are you sure it's him? He's the one that will help us when the time comes?" King Lewis needed to be sure. If what Strand was advised of the coming threat was true, he would need the help of this magician.

Strand studied the man in front of him, still working out in his mind how to interact with this once-boy as king. He hadn't been needed in the advisor role much since the last king. King Lewis

Edwards of Ethas was in his late thirties, but aside from the grey forming in his brown beard, one would think he was ten years younger. He stood just over six feet tall; his brown hair was wavy and worn at shoulder length. He was the spitting image of his grandfather, broad shoulders and all. He had taken the throne when his father passed fifteen years earlier.

"Yes, Sire. He will need training; he isn't aware yet he has these powers. But I felt something in him, something I haven't felt since Colvin."

"Colvin?" the king asked.

"Yes, he was the one who helped bring about the peace with your grandfather. Nobody has seen him in decades. There are rumours he visited your father once, though I am not sure what the meeting was for. In his absence, this young man will be what we need."

King Lewis stared at the short man, "What is our next step?"

"I will keep an eye on him for a few days to determine when will be the right time to talk to him. Until then, Lewis, please remember you cannot speak of this to anyone." Addressing the king informally was common when they were alone together, considering their longtime relationship.

"I understand, I don't want to." the king was interrupted by a knock on the door. "Come in."

The door opened and a regal-looking lady

walked through. She was of average height, but that was all that was average about her. She had long flowing red hair reaching the small of her back, and eyes the colour of a summer blue sky. Her hair was braided and tied with a white silk ribbon that matched the flowing evening gown that barely revealed her perfect hourglass figure.

Strand nodded, "Good evening, Your Majesty." His familiarity didn't extend to the queen.

"Strand, it is very nice to see you." The queen looked at her husband. "My love, are you coming to bed soon?"

"Yes, Reva, I will be there shortly." Lewis crossed the room to his lovely wife and kissed her on her forehead. "We just have a few more things to discuss and I will be on my way."

Reva nodded and turned to leave the door she came in. After the door closed, Lewis turned and looked around the room they were in. This was his private office, added by his father after he took the crown. It was known to exist only by a few: Strand, Reva, himself, and the head of the staff.

The simple, spare room was used to ensure prying ears wouldn't hear sensitive information. It was about thirty feet square. A book shelf covered the wall to the right of the door; a red couch and three brown chairs occupied the center of the room surrounding a round stone table, and on the wall with the door hung a large tapestry with the kingdom's crest. The wall across from the bookshelves had a waist-high table for drinks, food, and candles.

"Back to what we were discussing," said the king. "I don't want to cause any panic to anyone. How can we ensure he won't know you're observing him?"

"The same way we made sure those men who saw the soldiers coming in the western gate didn't remember. I do what I am good at," Strand said with a smirk.

"Yes, little man, you do. Which is how you get in and out of my palace!" They both laughed. "How much time do you guess we have to prepare?"

Strand walked over to the couch and sat down, placing his staff on the table in front of him. He looked up at the king, who still stood by the door. "A year, maybe. The Augur's powers are only clear within weeks of events. Unexpected things can't change what is to come, but they *can* change the time in which it happens."

"Let's hope if anything 'unexpected' happens, it works in our favour to prolong it. I could use as much time as possible to prepare for this." The king's voice betrayed his sense of worry. "I will be sending messengers to the other kingdoms tomorrow; we need to work together if we are to survive this."

"Go to your beautiful wife, Sire. I will leave shortly. I have a few more things I want to go over before I leave." Strand stood and walked over to the king, placed a hand on his forearm and looked up at him. "We will do what we must to get through this."

"Let's hope it's enough," said Lewis as he turned and opened the door his wife had gone though. He took one more look at the small man he was placing so much hope on, walked through the door and closed it.

Strand turned and walked back over to the table and picked up his staff. It was as tall as him and had what looked like a skeleton hand holding a purple orb. He walked over to the wall on the far side of the room, across from the door. It was empty aside from two candle sconces.

Facing the wall, he held up his staff and touched the wall with the orb, which began to glow. As it got brighter, the stone of the wall looked as if it began to swirl counter-clockwise, until it started to open up from the center of the swirl. A yellow glow streamed from the opening. As it grew large enough for Strand to walk through, he could see a large fire on the other side.

Strand stepped through and the hole closed behind him. He stood in an underground cave, with a large fire in the center of a room that was at least twenty times the size of the room he had just left, with the ceiling even higher.

"*Did you find the boy?*" came a voice in Strand's head. It was not the voice of a human, but something more. It was strong, but feminine.

"Yes," he replied out loud. "He was right

where you said he would be. The power I felt is unlike anything, even his father."

"We need to ensure we move with caution." The voice came in Strand's head again. *"We need him and cannot afford to lose him to his past. His future is more important than he could know."*

"King Lewis is reaching out to the other kingdoms to gain alliance. That will take some time, without any interference." Strand knew there were some things magicians shouldn't interfere with; forging alliances was one of them.

"If we must, we will find a way to share my visions with them. What is coming is more important than any one person. It cannot happen again."

Strand knew what the Augur spoke of, but it was so long ago and not spoken of for many centuries. The library on Bone Isle kept the history of Cruconia for the magicians to study. The Council of Magicians maintained it in the fortress there.

"When he is ready, the boy must be taken to Bone Isle to study and be made ready for what is to come."

"Agreed. I will be off now, there is much to be done." Strand turned back to the wall he had just come through, held his staff up again, and touched the wall. This time, when the hole opened, he stepped onto a cliff overlooking the ocean.

Strand stood there watching the ocean crash against the rocks below him. He was going over everything from the last few weeks in his mind. The Augur giving him the warning of what was coming, convincing King Lewis to take action, and finding Gevan – it was a lot, but it was just the beginning. After a century of peace, mortals knew only what had been passed down in each kingdom about what really happened. Strand was sure those legends didn't match either. Very few people knew even a portion of the truth.

Colvin was the most powerful sorcerer Strand had ever met. He was more than a magician; he was able to master any skill he attempted. Most magicians had only a skill or two.

Strand had the ability to read the minds of others, to an extent, and the ability to influence the thoughts or memories of a person. This was how he had helped get the soldiers in Ethas palace grounds. The group of men was "suggested" to forget what they saw. The staff Strand wielded, allowing him to transport between places, wasn't one of his own powers; it was a gift of the Augur.

The wind began to pick up, Strand turned and walked up the slope away from the cliff toward a simple stone house. On the front were two windows with a door in between. Smoke was coming from the chimney in the center of the roof, and as he stepped up to the door, the smell of something cooking hit his nose.

He paused and felt the familiar presence of someone he hadn't seen in a long time. With a smirk, he turned the doorknob and pushed open the door to greet his unexpected visitor.

∞ ∞ ∞

Gevan jumped awake. He suddenly remembered the little man he had met on the street. A short man with white hair and long white beard, standing about five feet tall.

He now recalled seeing him walking away down the street, where before he hadn't seen the stranger. He wasn't sure what was real and what was a dream. Who was that strange little man? How had he known where Gevan was going that night?

Gevan laid back down and stared at the ceiling, thinking of Harry and hoping he would see him again the next day. He rolled over on his left side and closed his eyes; he needed to get back to sleep, as he had a large delivery when he got up.

He let his mind wander back to his desire to travel and see as much of Cruconia as he could. What else was out there? Gevan slowly fell back to sleep.

Chapter 4

Gevan's morning delivery was uneventful. There were still practices going on in the palace yard, but they seemed a little more organized today than the day before. At the far end of the yard were rows of hay stacked with a bull's eye on them. Some of the soldiers were practicing archery. Gevan could tell some of them had never held a bow before. Another group was being shown how to make arrows out of tree branches.

Gevan was in the cart riding back to the bakery, lost in thought. The bakery was about half a mile from the gate, down a winding road past the pond where he got the feathers for his bed, and then a block into the village.

Gevan pulled up at the bakery, a two-story building on a corner of the block. The second story was the attic Gevan's bedroom was in. The front half, which didn't have a second story over it, was the store front. It was painted a dark green with black shutters on the windows. In the back was the kitchen, a formal sitting room, two bed-rooms, and the bathroom. Behind the building was the yard, with a stable for the horse and cart.

The entrance for the personal quarters was on the side and in the back. He turned right, down the side of the bakery, and then left in behind to pull the cart into the yard. He climbed off the cart and walked back to close the gate behind him.

As he was about to pull the gate closed, he saw the man he had met from the alley across the street. Gevan closed his eyes, counted to three, and opened them.

"What the…!" Gevan shouted as he jumped back. Strand was standing right in front of him.

"Sorry to startle you, young man. I intended to be a little more cautious when meeting you, but when I realized you could see me across the street, I figured it was time."

"Who are you?" was all Gevan could ask, even though he had many more questions. Questions like how did he know where Gevan was going last night, and why didn't Gevan see him walking away? How did he remember it early this morning?

"My name is Strand, and I have been looking for you. There are things I need to tell you, but now is not the time. I think you should forget seeing me today." Strand's voice dropped to a lower register as he looked deeply and penetratingly into Gevan's eyes, using his mental power to erase the meeting.

"Forget we met? Things to tell me?" Gevan was visibly irritated, and stepped toward the short man. "Are you following me? What do you want?"

Strand stared up at Gevan and realized with a sinking feeling that for the first time, his powers were useless on someone. Only Colvin had been immune to Strand's power, and even then only after Colvin had grown into his full strength. He hadn't expected this. Simply easing into this boy's life would be impossible now.

"Calm down, I am not here to cause any ill. We merely have some … common acquaintances I would like to talk to you about at some point." Strand was trying to keep the situation calm so as not to ruin his chances of Gevan trusting him.

"Oh, we do?" Gevan asked as he took a few steps back. "And would you like to come in to discuss these acquaintances?"

"Now is not a good time, but maybe we can arrange a time to meet away from your home? Possibly tomorrow after your delivery to the palace?" Strand didn't want to discuss anything with the chance of Vita or Lily overhearing. "By the pond up the road tomorrow?"

Before Gevan could answer, he heard his mother call from the back door. "Gevan, are you out here?" He turned to look and saw his mother calling from inside the house. When he turned to talk to the short man, he was gone.

"Gevan?" he heard again, and turned to see his mother just outside the door, looking at him.

"I'm just closing the gate, Mother," replied

Gevan distractedly.

"How was the delivery? Any problems?"

"No, Mother. Shorty requested the same amount of bread for tomorrow, and they all said thanks for the extra cookies." Gevan closed the gate and turned to walk back to his mother. "Mother, have you seen a man about this tall," he motioned with a hand to the middle of his chest, "with white short hair and long white beard around?"

"No, why?"

"No reason, I just saw him a time or two. I think he may be new in town." Gevan wasn't sure what to say about who the strange man was.

Vita looked at her son. He was not able to completely hide the concerned look on his face, but she didn't ask. "We do have boats coming in all the time from Fraycia and occasionally from Abareth. He could be a visitor."

"That's probably it. I will get the local deliveries on the cart and then I will get back out of here." Gevan didn't have the room to put them all on the cart with the larger delivery to the palace.

"Thank you, Gevan." Vita reached up and kissed her son on the right cheek, pulled back and touched it with her hand. She turned and went over to the garden of herbs and spices she maintained at the end of pathway into the back.

She was very good at gardening, able to keep her garden from failing even in the worst weather. They didn't get harsh winters this far south, but even on those rare days where there was frost, she was able to keep the plants well by covering them and caring for them.

Gevan had asked his mother once why she didn't become a spice merchant. Vita had responded only that there wasn't enough room in the back. She grew just enough for the family's meals; any extra she gave to friends. With her knack at it, Gevan though she could have done well at selling spices and flowers.

Gevan stood there for a minute, fondly watching his mother work in the garden. Something about Strand being there, and the way his mother was just a bit sentimental, had put Gevan in a bit of shocked state. Something was happening. He was getting a feeling like he had from his dreams. Something was coming, but dread didn't fully explain it. He was afraid.

∞∞∞

Gevan finished putting the horse in the stable and feeding her. He pulled the cart into the shed and closed the door, then he walked over to make sure the gate was locked. As he headed to the back door, he stopped and looked up to the sky. It was still light out, but evening was setting in. He had had a long day, but he felt more anxious than tired. He let out a sigh and went inside.

Inside the door was the long hallway to the kitchen. The first room on the right was his mother's bedroom. It used to be his and his sister's, since it was the largest, but when he moved to the attic, Lily wanted their mother to have the larger room.

Just past his mother's room on the right was the bathroom. On the left was his sister's bedroom, then the sitting room. Both were partially under his bedroom, as was a portion of the kitchen. Then it opened up to the large kitchen in the center of the first floor. A fireplace on the right helped heat the water tank above the bathroom in the attic. On the left was one of the ovens that helped heat Gevan's room, and next to the ovens in the corner was the ladder to his room.

On the adjacent wall was the door to the outside. The large table for eating and cooking sat in the center of the room. The sinks were on the opposite wall of the outside door, with a cooler on the far left of the sinks and another two ovens next to the fireplace. Across from the hall were more counters, cabinets, and the door to the storefront.

"Hi Gevan, did you have a good day?" Lily stopped cleaning the dishes and looked at her brother. "I know it was more than normal and you have no help. We have Minna at least."

"It was ok, thank you, Sis. Where is Minna?" He thought she would still be there helping with the large orders they had each day now.

"She went home to get some fresh clothes. We are setting up a second bed in my room since she will be staying here a few days a week until we slow down."

"Is Mother around?"

"She's resting until Minna gets back. Sit down, I will get you some stew she made." Lily reached up on the shelf to the left of the sink and pulled down a bowl. The pot was in the sink, still steaming as she filled the bowl.

As she turned around to take it to the table, Gevan was sitting down at the far end. "Thank you, I'm starved." Lily set the bowl in front of him. It was filled with carrots, potatoes, and rabbit. "This smells wonderful, can you pass me a roll?" He pointed to the bowl of rolls at the end of the table by the sink.

Lily winked at him. "Catch!" was her only warning as she tossed the roll. He caught it with his right hand; it almost was out of his reach.

"You really never learned how to aim right! Good thing Mother wasn't in here to see it." They both laughed.

After Gevan was done eating, he went out back and brought in all the baskets so they could be filled again for tomorrow's delivery. He stacked them between the fireplace and the table and the counter on the opposite side of the table, so they weren't in the walkway to the ovens.

"I am going up to my room for a bit. If you need anything when Mother gets up or when Minna returns, just holler up at me." Gevan yawned and turned toward the ladder.

"Will do, brother." Lily watched her brother climb the ladder to his room. They were all busier than normal; she wondered if there was someone to help out Gevan in his deliveries.

The rumors of the men in the palace were filling everyone's conversation now. With people going in and of the gates all day and the obvious noise of the practice, it wasn't a secret any longer. Everyone was getting busier now.

∞ ∞ ∞

Gevan was sitting on a log near a what seemed to be a burned-down village. Rain poured down around him, the soot from the burnt buildings mixing with dirt and making swirls of black and brown in the puddles forming at his feet. He looked up and saw bodies on the streets, seemingly frozen in a running position, but black as coal. They had been burned in place so quickly there was no time to hide or even scream in agony.

Horrified, he raised his hand in front of his face. It wasn't wet at all. He stood up and saw that his clothes also were dry. As he turned around, he realized he was in the middle of the village, with the destruction all around him. A smell of campfire and burned meat filled his nose.

Gevan noticed movement near a building close to him. As he walked over, he saw a man kneeling in the middle of what must have been the village square. As he walked closer, the man put his left hand on the side of a well and lifted himself. He wore a dark robe with the hood pulled over his face. As he stood, he looked over at Gevan, "How are you here? You shouldn't be here."

"Gevan!" hollered Lily, and Gevan jumped awake. "You have a visitor down here."

"I will be right down." Gevan could still smell the charred wood and humans in his nostril. He felt sick. This dream was more realistic than any other. Where was this place and who was the man? What did he mean, he wasn't supposed to be there?

He sat on the edge of his bed and put his head in his hands. Rubbing his eyes, he stood up and walked over to the sink next to the ladder. He splashed some water on his face and looked into the mirror, the water was running down his face, and just stared at himself. After a moment of trying to get his mind clear, he wiped his face with a towel and went to the ladder and climbed down.

When he reached the bottom and turned around, he was face to face with Harry. "Good evening, Harry," he said with a huge smile.

"Hi Gevan. I didn't see you around town today, so I came by here. Hope that is ok." Harry replied with a half-grin.

Before Gevan could answer, Lily jumped in

and asked, "Harry, would you like something to drink? Ale, water, juice?"

"No thank you, Lily," Harry replied. He looked at Gevan, "Do you have time to go for a walk?"

"Um, I think… Yes, I would like that." Gevan stumbled his reply. He didn't know why he was so tongue-tied around Harry. He knew he liked him; he hadn't really ever liked anyone before.

He turned and waved to Lily, who just smiled. They went out the side door of the kitchen to the street. Once outside, Harry took Gevan's hand and they started to walk east toward the shoreline.

"When I met you last night, there was something about you. Something I haven't felt before." Harry said as he looked at Gevan. "My gut tells me you feel the same."

"I do, but I know nothing about you. Where you're from, what you do, or even how long are you staying."

Harry stopped and looked at Gevan. "Well the last part I cannot answer yet, but I am from Fraycia and am," he paused, "a negotiator of sorts."

"A negotiator. Well, that is interesting. Is that why you are here?" asked Gevan.

"No, it's more of a vacation. I wanted to have some time to re-evaluate my career. I am looking at a promotion but I'm not sure I want it." Harry began walking again, still holding Gevan's hand.

They walked in silence for a while until they reached the Bay of Likor. It was a coast of steep cliffs with only a few paths down the almost one hundred feet of rock, best travelled during the daylight. They sat down on a large rock not much more than an arm's length from the edge, overlooking the bay.

"So, tell me about you, Gevan. What do you like? What do you do other than work at the bakery?"

As he looked at Harry on his right, the breeze from the bay moving his hair slightly, Gevan contemplated his reply. He knew he wanted adventure, but what was adventure to Harry? He wanted to travel, more than just local and neighbouring islands. He wanted to see what was out there, beyond what he knew already.

"I want to travel. I want to figure out what is out there we don't know about yet." Gevan was a bit shy in admitting this; he hadn't told anyone this before, not even Jack.

"I am sure there is a lot we don't know, and even more than we could imagine," Harry replied. "I haven't been anywhere but here and Fraycia. I had plans to do some travel north, but my father recently passed away and now with all the responsibilities from his passing, there has been no time." Harry looked out over the bay, and then felt Gevan's hand on his left thigh.

"I am sorry about your father. I never knew mine; he was gone before I was born. Our mother doesn't really talk about him. She moved here after he passed and started the bakery."

"I am not sure which is harder," Gevan continued, "not knowing your father, or knowing him and losing him. One leaves you with so many questions, and the other with so much grief." Gevan's voice trailed off; Harry was silent.

Gevan hesitantly asked the next question. "And what of your mother?"

"She passed away when I was born." Sudden tears welled in Harry's eyes. Gevan truly regretted asking the question.

Seeing this in his face, Harry wiped a tear from his eye and leaned over to kiss Gevan on his cheek. "It's okay, don't regret asking me questions and getting to know me."

They sat on the rock and talked for what seemed hours. As the sun set behind them, and the chill off the water crashing down on the shores of bay below cut the heat of the summer, Harry put his arm around Gevan as Gevan laid his head on Harry's shoulder.

"We should head back," Gevan finally said. "We have had a lot of extra work with all the soldiers practicing at the palace the last few days. I am not sure if my mother needs help tonight or not."

Harry stood up and Gevan followed. "Is there anything I can do? I know my way around a kitchen, believe it or not. My mother passed away when we were young, and I spent some time hanging out with the kitchen staff as they cooked."

Gevan's eyes opened wide. "Kitchen staff, huh?"

Harry laughed, "Yes, we had a cook. Back to my offer."

"I appreciate it, but I think we are ok. A friend of Lily is helping us as well." Gevan took Harry's hand this time, and they began the walk back to the bakery. There wasn't much conversation on the way back, only a few comments about the surroundings and Gevan telling stories of growing up around here and his friend Jack.

Gevan reminded himself that he needed to talk to Jack about the soldiers and if there was anything he knew. He hadn't had the chance to go see him that day with all the deliveries. He thought to himself that he might sneak out later to go see Jack, if he was not needed at home.

Once they reached the door to the kitchen at home, Harry stopped and turned to Gevan. "I had a good time. When can I see you again?"

"Tomorrow? Dinner maybe? We can meet somewhere," Gevan said with excitement. It was getting easier to talk to Harry.

"Perfect. I will send a note on where after lunch tomorrow. You should have it by the time you are done with your deliveries." He reached up and put his right hand behind Gevan's head, while still holding Gevan's hand with his left. He pulled Gevan close and gave him a tender kiss on his lips.

Gevan closed his eyes and felt the tickle of

Harry's dark blond hair on his chin, the softness of his lips, and the warmth of his breath from his nose.

When Harry pulled back, Gevan opened his eyes and said, "Good night. I will see you tomorrow." Gevan smiled.

Harry turned and walked to the corner, took a look back, and then turned left to head down to the boarding house. Gevan turned, opened the door, and went inside to the kitchen.

Chapter 5

Strand closed the door behind him. After his visit with Gevan in the morning, he had gone to Bone Isle to seek information in the magician's library kept there. He was still surprised by his inability to use his powers on Gevan.

Placing his cloak on a hook next to the door and leaning his staff against the wall next to it, he stopped and looked around the main room of his cabin. It was the kitchen, sitting room, and dining room all in one. The room opened up to the right; under the window on the same wall was an orange couch with two matching chairs facing it and a short table in the center. Behind the chairs was a wooden square dining table with a chair on each side. The far one was pulled out toward the sink and fireplace that was beside it. On the right was the door to his bedroom, and another door down that wall led to the bathroom.

There was no sign of the unexpected visitor he had come home to late last night, except that the warming pot of stew that had been waiting from him was being reheated. There were two bowls on the sink next to the fireplace, with spoons and napkins next to them.

As Strand walked toward the fireplace to check on the stew, he heard the door open behind him. He turned to see a figure walk through, wearing a red long cloak with the hood pulled all the way forward.

Strand turned back to the fire. "I thought you might have left again." Comings and goings used to be a common theme.

"No, I just went out to bring more firewood next to the door. My dear Strand, I know I have not always stuck around long, but I never left without saying goodbye." The figure pulled back the hood to reveal her strikingly jet-black hair, pulled back in a pony tail showing off her pointed ears. Her light purple eyes sparkled from the light of the fireplace. She took off her robe and put it on a hook to the left of the door, next to the couch.

She walked over to Strand in what seemed more of a gentle glide, her slim body and small bosom draped by a white silky gown trimmed in gold around the plunging neckline and sleeve cuffs. It was wrapped and held closed by a golden tie around her waist.

She stopped in front of Strand. She was no taller than he, and she looked him directly in the eyes with a frank appraisal. She stroked his long white beard with her right hand and said, "Now the stew should be warmed, please sit and I will serve us."

Strand turned and sat in the chair, which was already pulled out. It faced the door and was where he usually preferred to sit. "You didn't have much to say last night. I still am not sure why you have come to visit unexpectedly."

The woman placed the bowls in front of each of their seats. She took the napkins and spoons off the counter and placed them on the table and then sat down to his right, facing the expanse of wall opposite of the bedroom. She gazed at the wall for a moment. "When will you ever hang something on that empty wall?"

"Probably never. Now let's stop stalling and discuss why you are here." Strand put the spoon in his stew and stirred it mindlessly while looking at the woman. "Avae, it must be important to bring you all the way here."

Avae's mouth pursed in a slight smile. "My love, there has been some talk amongst the different elven tribes. Our queen has heard you have been visiting the Augur and have been given a warning. She has asked that I come and find out if our people have anything to be concerned about." She paused, and then raised a graceful hand to stroke his cheek and then gently kissed him on the opposite cheek. "And I missed you terribly. It has been too long since we have spent time together."

Strand looked at her striking purple eyes and thought for a minute. "There is something coming, a danger far worse than this world has faced in a long time," he finally replied. "It will affect the elven tribes, but most significantly and dangerously, your tribe, my dear. I have not all the information, but the Augur has put me on the path of one who will be our best hope of surviving and overcoming this threat."

Avae was staring at Strand with a look he had seen very few times; he knew she was agitated, but moreso worried. Avae stood and made her way next to the fireplace. Staring into the fire, she asked, "When were we to be made aware of this threat?"

Strand walked over to her and wrapped his arms around her waist from behind. "My beautiful Avae, I only found out recently. I have been delivering word of this for the Augur so others may begin preparing. I was to come see you very soon. I would have come sooner if I could have. As you are here now, I need to know more on how your people need to prepare. If you can." The last was said in a bit lower voice; then he kissed her on the back of the neck.

Avae did not pull away, but her gaze remained on the fire. "What can you tell me of this threat? Anything I can take back to my Queen?" Avae's concern was now apparent in her tone.

"Not much, I am afraid. Let's finish eating, and I will tell you what I do know." Strand took Avae's hand and walked her back to the table.

They finished eating while they discussed what he knew. He told her of Gevan, his visits with King Lewis, and his plans to reach out to the other two kingdoms. They eventually moved over to the couch. Strand sat on one end, and Avae laid in his lap and looked up at him as they continued to talk about what was coming.

After hearing what Strand knew, she knew what to expect. This wasn't the first time Cruconia had faced a threat like this, but the last time, the land had only barely survived. Even then, the survival came at great loss and upheaval to all the kingdoms. She wasn't sure this time would be any better.

Finally, they were talked out. They sat a while gazing at the fire. Then Avae stood. "Come, my love. Let's go to bed and get some rest." She reached out a hand to him.

"Go on ahead," Strand replied. "I will be there shortly. I have a few things to work out in my head first."

Avae bent to kiss Strand gently on the forehead and walked over into the bedroom, closing the door behind her. Strand knew there was more she needed to know, but he didn't have enough of the information to tell her. His research today had led only to more questions, questions he needed to ask the Augur. The Augur had been around centuries longer than he or Colvin, long before the library at Bone Isle had kept any records.

Strand stood up and walked over to pick up his staff by the door. He turned and walked to the blank wall. He stopped and stared it for a moment. He had put a painting on the wall after Avae visited last time. After receiving the staff from the Augur, the first time he used it the painting was thrown off the wall and broken. The displacement of the portal seemed to have a slight backdraft. From then on, he had used the staff only on empty walls.

He picked up his staff and placed it against the wall with his left arm and watched as the purple orb began to glow bright. The wall began spinning counterclockwise.

Suddenly Strand felt a someone grab his right arm. Startled, he spun.

"If you're going somewhere, I am going with you, my love." Avae said with a smile.

Strand kissed her on the lips and looked back at the wall as the swirl began to open the hole in the center. The glowing light of the large fire was familiar to Strand, but new to Avae. When it was large enough, they both walked through, and the hole closed behind them.

They entered a large dark cavern, with just a big fire in the center of it casting dancing shadows on the far wall. It didn't seem to give off any smoke.

Then Strand heard a voice in his head, *"Hello again Strand, and welcome, Avae."*

Strand looked at Avae and she was staring at him. He knew she heard the voice as well.

"Greetings on behalf of my Queen," replied Avae aloud.

"Please give her my regards. It has been far too

long, but it is nice to finally meet you after all these years."

"Avae has joined me to, well, I am sure you know." Strand knew the Augur's power of premonition and was sure she was aware of their arrival before he even knew they were coming.

"Yes, there are things your clan must know about the coming threat."

"Why is this happening now? Who is this threat?" Avae seemed to ask anxiously. If she was impressed at meeting the Augur, it didn't show to Strand.

As if searching for something, Avae looked around as she spoke to a voice in her head, but not a physical being besides Strand was around. "What battle must we prepare for?"

"My dear, I understand your sense of urgency," the voice replied, still projecting in both their heads, *"but understand we must be cautious of our approach. We believed this threat was not able to come again after the last battle, thought to have been banished. We cannot make that mistake again."*

Strand just stood by, letting Avae and the Augur have this discussion, but he could see Avae's concern.

"The once-banished is finding its way back into our world, and it is growing more powerful and deadly. Strand has already begun warning the humans, and I need you to warn your clan and those of the Yellow Mist."

"What are we to do?" Avae seemed to be

calming down.

"You must protect the Red Lake at all costs. If the mountain falls, so does the land you call home. What your clan protects is more important than is known."

"The barriers and protection spells are quite impressive," commented Strand.

"Yes, for human and other mortal beings. For those coming, more will need to be done to deter any intrusion."

Avae asked, "how can we do that?"

"It must be protected as is Old Fraycia, only stronger."

Strand looked at Avae. He knew only one sorcerer knew how that was done. He also knew there was only one person right now that could even possibly do the same.

"For now, there isn't anything else I can tell you."

"Thank you. I will speak with my Queen and do what we must." Avae looked at Strand, her purple eyes wide and glowing in the fire light.

"Then I bid you both farewell."

Both Avae and Strand said their good-byes and Strand opened up a portal to leave the cavern. They both stepped through.

∞∞∞

The Smark family sat around the dining room table, seemingly large with only the four of them there. It was a dark wooden dining table, with three chairs on each side and an armchair at each end. They had padded seats and back, upholstered in a fine green silk. It was surrounded by two side tables on the long sides of the room, with doors on both ends. One led to the kitchen and the other to the sitting room.

Tomis sat at the head of the table near the kitchen, with his wife to his right and two children to his left. His eldest son, Jack, had been completing his higher studies and helping out a sick uncle recently. The younger son, Patrick, was only five years old and just now beginning school.

As they were finishing up the roast duck with only bones left on their plates, Jack decided to bring up what had been on everyone's mind around the village. "Father, I was with Gevan last night, and he mentioned all the soldiers practicing at the palace. He wanted to ask what it was all about, but all I knew wouldn't be any more than he does already. What is going on?"

Tomis looked at his wife, Gwen, then their son Patrick. "Gwen, would you take the little guy and get him cleaned up?" He didn't want to discuss anything in front of his youngest.

"Of course. Would either of you like anything more before we go?" Gwen asked. Both shook their heads no and thanked her. She stood up and walked around behind Tomis to the other side of the table, picked up Patrick, and left through the door to the sitting room.

Tomis paused until he was sure Gwen and his youngest were out of earshot. He began fiddling with a fork he was staring at, and then looked up at Jack. "Son, there is not much I know yet to be able to tell you. King Lewis has worked out a deal with some of the surrounding dukes to train his men in what he called an exercise."

Jack was watching his father's face closely. "That doesn't really make sense. We haven't had any exercises that I can remember. We've been at peace for almost a century. Who are we going to need to be in practice for?"

Tomis looked at his son; it was like looking in the mirror when he was younger. "I understand. My sudden promotion, although welcome, was a surprise. I think there is more going on, but I don't have any more right now to tell you." He really didn't. He hadn't been given more than the fact that his promotion was to help organize the men. He was suspicious himself, but he didn't want his son to know that right now.

"I am done with my advanced studies now," Jack said after a moment. "I think it may be time I figure out my next step. The men in our family have always been members of the Royal Guard, usually at a younger age than I am now. It is time I continued that tradition." It sounded to Tomis like more of a decision than a question.

"Son, you are correct about the tradition. Are you sure this is what you want to do? Is there nothing else which interests you?" Tomis' question was more out of concern than desire to break the tradition.

Jack met his father's gaze confidently. "I am sure, father. I can put my political studies to good use, use the knowledge to maintain the relationships between the kingdoms. I have studied the history of all three kingdoms in depth." Jack's mind raced ahead. "We have had so little contact since the war, besides the trade agreements. The royals of each kingdom haven't even been together for decades. Does anyone even know what the Queen Mabantra of Abareth or the twin Princes of Fraycia look like?"

Tomis couldn't argue with his son's reasoning. In fact, the royals of the kingdoms had met only once since the war a hundred years ago. The last two generations had never met at all. What was known of how they looked came only from stories; there were not even any paintings or drawings that had been shared between royals. Only the occasional duke or duchess from the region had actually visited multiple kingdoms.

Finally, Tomis sighed. "Very well, Jack. I will speak with the head of the Royal Guard and hear what he suggests."

"Thank you." Jack stood and carried the rest of the plates to the kitchen.

Just as Tomis was about to stand up, Gwen returned. "Patrick is in his room. What happened here?"

Tomis waved at her to sit down; she took Jack's seat. "He wants to join the Royal Guard," Tomis said. "He thinks he can bring a better relationship to the kingdoms through his political studies."

Gwen reached over and took her husband's left hand in hers. "He was going to follow your footsteps somehow," she said gently. "He is closer to being like you than either of us want to admit." She thought for a moment. "This position he seeks, is it even something existing? Will any of the kingdoms even want to build a closer relationship after all this time?" Gwen knew some of the history of the kingdoms were distant, based on Tomis' position.

"I just don't know, but with all that's happening right now, we may need him." Tomis was referring to the sudden influx of men in training.

Gwen stood up and reached over to kiss Tomis on his forehead, but before she could he scooted his chair back and twirled her to sit in his lap. He looked up at her long blonde hair, pulled back to show her fair complexion and hazel eyes. "I love you, my beautiful wife." He pulled her head close and gave her a long kiss, paying attention to how soft her lips were.

"Well, keep acting like that tonight and we will have another mouth to feed soon." She laughed, stood up and headed toward the kitchen to help Jack clean up. As she walked away, Tomis playfully swatted her on the left butt cheek. She turned and smiled at him but kept walking.

"Maybe we will," he said loudly as she left the room.

Chapter 6

Gevan nodded to the guard as he exited the palace gate after his morning delivery. It was back to being only one guard on duty, and Gevan noticed there were only half as many men in the yard. Shorty had told him they were in a training room in the palace, probably doing some sort of tactical training.

He briefly watched the soldiers in the yard practicing making and breaking camp. It seemed they were having a contest to see which team was quicker. They were raising tents, starting campfires, breaking down tents, putting out the fires, and packing everything up. It seemed very repetitive, but Gevan figured it was a necessary skill.

As he drove down the path, he pulled over by the pond where Strand was going to meet him this morning. Gevan still wasn't sure why he was even willing to meet this odd, short man. Besides the feeling of fear, there was a curiosity behind his two meetings with the old man.

He parked the horse and cart near a log by the pond and stepped down. The horse began to graze on the grass and didn't seem to mind the break. From the log he could see the eastern gate and the guard outside keeping an eye on things.

For fifteen minutes Gevan sat and pondered why he was here. Why was he waiting, and how long was he supposed to wait? Had Strand already come by and left because Gevan wasn't here? How would he even know when Gevan was done with his delivery?

Gevan decided he wasn't going to wait in any longer and he stood up to get back on the cart. But then, from the corner of his eye, he saw something shimmering on the wall about a hundred feet from the gate. It seemed as if the bricks were moving, almost swirling in the sunlight. After a few seconds, a dark circle began to form in the middle. It opened up large enough for Strand to step through.

Gevan was stunned. It was not like anything he had ever seen. It seemed the guard hadn't seen anything like it either; as Strand stepped out of the hole, the guard drew his sword from his left side and began to run toward the short man who had appeared out of nowhere. Strand stroked his beard and looked around, taking in his surroundings as the circle and swirl disappeared behind him. Noticing the soldier who was about to reach him, he calmly turned toward him.

With sword drawn, the soldier stopped and confronted Strand. Suddenly, the soldier stood up straight and sheathed his sword. He nodded curtly at the short man in front of him and then turned to walk back to the gate. Once at the gate, the guard stepped inside the archway of the gate and turned to face the outside of the palace and just posed there, standing still.

Strand walked the approximately four hundred feet to where the pond was. Gevan was still standing there in awe of not only how Strand appeared, but also his interaction with the guard. Who was this silver-haired man and what did he want? What had Gevan gotten himself into?

As Strand approached, Gevan unthinkingly took two steps back. Strand frowned. "Relax, young man. I am not here to harm you in any way. I am here to talk and ask for your help; in turn I will help you."

"What can I do to help you?" Gevan asked, still keeping his distance. "More importantly, how did you just appear? What was that?" Gevan had many more questions he wanted to ask.

"You will get these answers and many more in time. I'm sure I have a lot more questions, too. First, I am a magician of sorts. My staff here," Strand raised it up to show it more closely to Gevan, "gives me the ability to transport to places I have been before. I came to the wall, since I haven't been here at the pond and didn't want to end up in the middle of it." Strand chuckled a bit. "I don't have the ability to dry myself instantly." Gevan did not chuckle.

"What about the guard – how did you get

him to go back to the gate?" Gevan asked, pointing to the guard, who still stood as motionless as a statue. Was he even breathing? Gevan couldn't tell for sure.

"I have the ability to read minds, or short spurts of thoughts, anyway. I can also make suggestions to people. That is why the first night you couldn't remember me well; I had suggested you forget the details. You shouldn't have remembered me at all." The last sentence was said with some curiosity.

"But I did remember you. Not well, though. Not until that night anyway, I woke up recalling it all," Gevan confessed.

"Yes, and then the other day I couldn't make you forget again." The old magician was frowning. "You are more powerful than I expected you to be." The straightforward, factual tone of his voice was unsettling.

"Powerful?" Gevan laughed loudly. "Me? No, I am merely the son of a baker. My mother might be magical in the kitchen, but there is nothing magical about me."

"I am not expecting this to come from your mother. The power inside of you is from your father." Strand wasn't sure how Gevan was going to take this information, but time was not on his side to break the news as gently as he had planned. With his inability to use his powers on Gevan, there was no point in beating around the bush. Strand plowed on. "If my suspicions are correct, and they usually are, you are much more than a magician. You have the potential to be a great sorcerer as your father is."

Gevan stared at him, mouth agape. "Sorcerer? I think you have the wrong person." Gevan sat back down on the log and looked at the pond, his mind spinning. The water was calm, and there were half a dozen geese gliding across the surface. They were large birds, about three feet tall when standing and walking around. They were grey in colour with streaks of blue on their wings and tails.

Strand sat down next to Gevan. "I assure you I have the right person. Your father's power helped bring about the peace we now enjoy. With your help, we can continue to enjoy it."

"That was almost a century ago," Gevan said automatically. "That isn't even possible." He found it ridiculous he was expected to believe his father was alive a hundred years ago, let alone a sorcerer. "My father is dead."

Strand drew a long breath before continuing. "No. Your father hasn't been seen in decades, but he is surely alive. Those with abilities tend to live a much longer life, centuries even. The more power, the longer the life that is given, it seems. I am over two hundred years old myself." Strand looked at the disbelief in Gevan's eyes. "I know, I don't look a day over a hundred and fifty!"

With that, Gevan finally couldn't resist chuckling. Then his expression sobered.

"Say this is all true. What do you need from me?" Gevan wasn't sure what else to ask at this point; it all seemed too much to comprehend.

"You have been having feelings, dreams and sensing something. Am I right?" Strand knew from hearing Gevan's thoughts at their previous meeting that this was true.

Gevan stared suspiciously at the man sitting next to him. "Yes, I have. Some leave me filled with dread, some with fear, and others just uneasy. Sometimes I feel like there is something coming we need to get ready for." Gevan looked pensively out over the pond. "My mother has said they were just a result of eating too much too late and then sleeping. When they started happening while I was awake, like when we met yesterday, it became more worrying."

Strand sighed. It was worse than he had thought. Worse and better. He decided being up front was best. "Gevan, there is much to tell you about what you are feeling. We don't have the time right now to explain it all, but you need to know this." He drew Gevan's gaze and met his eyes squarely. "You are right. There *is* something coming. Something we haven't seen in over a century on this world. If you are willing to explore what is inside of you and be trained, we have a chance to stop this."

"What about my father? He's alive?" Gevan was getting more comfortable with Strand, but there were so many questions, and this all seemed so unreal. He had heard of magic before, but there wasn't mention of it in school, nor was it a common discussion among people. It seemed to be a myth some believed in and some did not. Similar to some people's belief in the gods.

"Your father was gone for many centuries," Strand answered. "Nobody knows where. He obviously showed up here almost twenty years ago," Strand couldn't avoid a sardonic smile, "but hasn't been seen again since. I knew him a long time ago, but where he is now, I do not know. Your mother may know more. But then, she may not even know about his powers."

"From what we've been told, our father passed away from an illness. Lily and I never knew who he was." Something clicked in Gevan's mind. "Wait! Does that mean Lily also has powers? She's a sorceress?"

"Not necessarily, it isn't always passed down the same. "Strand was choosing his words carefully; it was best not to burden the young man with the full truth just yet. "That seems true with you. You seem to have a stronger power of magic than your father. What that means, I don't know yet."

Strand looked at Gevan. He could see the confusion in the young man's eyes. "I know there are many questions and much to discuss. You need to realize, though – once you set out on this path, your life will never be as it is now. I will need you to come with me to explore what you can do and learn about the past of the kingdoms so you can prepare."

Gevan stared again at the pond and the geese swimming around. Then he looked back at the guard, still standing motionless. "I need to talk to my mother. When can we meet again?"

"In two days' time. I will find you; I have some things to take care of until then. Think carefully, and be careful who you share this with," Strand added as a warning. "We cannot involve too many yet."

"I understand. Thank you." Gevan stood and walked to the cart. He turned back to Strand, but again the old man was gone. Gevan wasn't shocked this time, but at least he could have said goodbye.

Then he looked over at the guard. He was walking around the entrance of the gate, moving freely again. Gevan climbed on the cart and headed home, his head cluttered with too much information – and even more questions.

∞∞∞

As Gevan entered the back of the house to load up the rest of the day's delivery, his mother was finishing up in the garden. Carrying a basket, she looked at him as she reached the back door, and paused.

"Are you well?" she asked with a look of

concern as her head tilted to the right.

Gevan climbed down from the cart and walked over to the back door, unsure what to say to her. He had so many questions. Did she know who his father was and that he was still alive?

"I am," was all he could say as he kissed her on the forehead. He figured it was best to get the deliveries done and get his thoughts in order before talking to her. Right now he didn't know what to think himself.

"I am going to load up the other deliveries and be back as soon as I can." He began to walk in the door but paused, and turned to his mother. "I have dinner plans tonight."

"Is this with the young man Lily said came by last night?" Vita and Lily were busy cooking when he had returned home the night before, after his walk with Harry. He didn't have a chance to talk about it with them; besides, Minna was around.

"Yes. I will talk to you more before I go tonight." He walked into the house and started gathering the baked goods and placing them in the baskets on the cart.

After he was done, he took the leftover empty baskets into the kitchen. They were already preparing the next day's order. They had become more efficient, and with the extra work, there was enough to pay Minna for her help. Business also seemed to be picking up outside the palace in the last few weeks.

Gevan turned the horse and cart around in the back drive and went out the gate, turning right to get to the corner. He turned right again and headed down toward the shore.

When he reached the Red Lake Tavern and went in with their order, the same short, balding man was behind the bar who had been there the other night. "Good afternoon," Gevan greeted him. "I have the bread order; you were here the other night bartending. I hadn't seen you before but was told it was your nephew was helping with service. My name is Gevan; my mother Vita owns the Twisted Feather bakery."

The man replied a bit dismissively, "Hello, I am Will. That was my brother's son, Philip. You can place the bread on the counter."

Trying to make conversation, Gevan asked, "Are you new around here?"

With a sigh, Will replied, "Yes. My brother is the owner of this place. Now unless you have more questions, I have work to do."

Gevan just smiled and wished him a good day. He took the baskets and walked back to the door, where he almost bumped into a slim, dark-haired man as he was about to come into the tavern. It was Philip, the nephew he had just ben discussing with Will.

"Pardon me, Philip." Gevan said as he patted the young man on this right shoulder.

"No, excuse me, sir. I wasn't watching where I was going. My uncle will be spastic if I am late."

Then he paused and looked at Gevan, "How did you know my name?"

"Your uncle just told me. I was in here a few nights ago with some friends and you were helping out."

"Ah, yes. My father and mother own the tavern and boarding house, they had two waitresses not show and my uncle insisted I help."

"Are you helping out again today. then?" The tavern was only open a little while and nobody was in there right now. Gevan didn't think it was busy enough to need more than one person.

"Not serving. I just finished school and my parents want me to learn the bartending. I would rather find something else, but they don't want me to sit around doing nothing until then." Philip's displeasure at bartending was obvious.

"Well if you're interested, we are looking for someone at the bakery to help with deliveries. It will keep you outside a lot, and you get to know much more of the town." Gevan had been wanting help with all the work of taking care of the horses and deliveries.

Philip pondered the offer. He was a bit taller than Gevan, yet slimmer, with brown hair and brown eyes. He would be considered handsome by most, but he was shy by nature. "Let me talk to my parents. "With my uncle here now, I am sure I can convince them. Can I come by the bakery later and talk to you?"

"Sure, that would be great. If I am not there

talk to my mother, Vita. You know were it is?"

"The top of this street, right? My mother told me the name was Twisted Feather, I think." Philip had been learning some information about the business since he finished school.

"That's it. You'd better get in there before your uncle goes looking for you," Gevan said with a smile, and they both chuckled.

∞ ∞ ∞

Gevan returned to the bakery and put the horse in the stable with the other one. They had two but used only one at a time to pull the cart on a daily basis, as it wasn't usually a heavy load. They were both brown with tan manes and tails. They were muscular animals and, when untrained, very temperamental. He fed them and ensured they had water. Then he backed the cart into the shed and locked up the gate to the yard.

He went inside, where his mother was sitting at the dining table drinking a cup of coffee while Minna and Lily finished the dishes. "Would you like a cup, Gevan?" Vita asked.

"I would love one!" he replied. He went into the bathroom to wash his hands, and when he returned his mother was waiting at the entrance of the kitchen with a cup for him and a cup for her.

"Let's go into the sitting room and talk for

a minute," She suggested. Devan took his cup of coffee and nodded. They entered the sitting room, which was just across from the bathroom. It was connected to Lily's bedroom and shared a chimney with the fireplace centered on the left wall.

It was a bit more formal than the rest of the house. There were two overstuffed red chairs on either side of the fireplace, with side tables next to each. On the wall opposite the door were two large windows with dark brown velvet drapes that could be pulled shut, and a wooden cabinet with glass doors displaying silver collectible figurines from Vita's parents. On the right was an extra-long couch, matching the chairs and marble-top low table in front. A low bench covered in brown leather sat opposite the couch between the table and fireplace.

Paintings covered the walls of the sitting room. The largest one, over the couch, was a piece land his grandparents once grew up on according to his mother. It didn't look like any place around here, though. The others were portraits of his ancestors; most he knew by relation as explained by his mother.

"Sit here next to me, son," Vita said softly as she sat on the bench facing the couch. "I know something was bothering you earlier; I could look at you and know it. What is it?"

Gevan pondered how much he wanted to ask his mother, and how much he wanted to tell her. He sat down and looked at her, then looked up at the large picture hanging above them. "Where is this picture from?"

"I've told you, where your grandparents grew up."

"Yes, but where is that? It doesn't look like anywhere around here I have seen." Gevan was stalling and prodding for information.

"It's a very long way from here. Now I know this is not what is bothering you." She knew she couldn't explain fully where the picture was painted from to Gevan, not now. If ever.

Gevan's gaze remained on the painting. "Remember the man I asked you about yesterday?"

Vita did remember. It wasn't the first time she had heard his description. "Yes, the visitor you saw."

"He wasn't a visitor. I guess you could say he is a traveller. It was the second time I saw him, the second time I have spoken to him." He looked at his mother and her expression changed. "The third time was today by the pond. He said he knows my father."

"Knew your father," Vita said gently.

"No, *knows* him. He said he is still alive. And there were so many other things he told me. I am still trying to believe and understand everything he told me."

Vita began to fidget with her blue apron over her simple yellow pullover dress. "What did he tell you?" She looked uncomfortable.

Gevan looked back at the painting. "He

said he had powers of sorts. That he was around and helped bring the peace we have had for the last century." He looked at his mother who had stopped fidgeting and was now staring at him. "I know, all this sounds like nonsense."

Vita stood up and walked around the bench to the door of the sitting room. She closed it and turned to look at Gevan. She untied her apron from behind and set it on the table next to the door. Then she walked back over to him and sat next to him. She put her hand on his right leg, "Go on."

Gevan was surprised at her suggestion that he continue. He had expected her to stop the conversation, be upset, or even deny it all. The last thing he expected was her to be calm.

He fumbled a bit for words. "He said I have powers too, more so he thinks than my father did, or does. He wants me to go with him to explore them. He said he will need me to help keep the peace."

His mother stood up again and walked around the bench, but this time she went to the wooden cabinet between the windows. At the very bottom she opened what seemed to be a secret door and pulled out a simple wooden box, then closed the door. She turned and walked back over to Gevan and handed him the box.

Gevan took the box and set it in his lap. Holding it gave him chills. He was overwhelmed with many sensations he had never felt, but seemed familiar somehow. He looked down at the box. It was light brown with was looked to be a map carved into the top of it. There wasn't any obvious way of opening it. Where did it come from? Had it always been there, hidden right in front of him his whole life?

His mother was watching him carefully. "I have never been able to open this. Your father said to give it to you should the day come you discover you have any abilities. Neither of us were sure you would gain any, but this was a precaution. What Strand told you is true."

Vita sat back down and looked at Gevan. "How did you know his name?" he asked.

"Your father talked to me about him a few times. He was a friend – *is* a friend of his. I didn't want to believe it was him you saw." Vita let out a big sigh. "There is much I should tell you, but it will take some time to explain it all."

"What about Lily? Will she also have abilities?"

"Most likely not." Vita hesitated. "Her father was not a sorcerer like yours was." This was the first time she let on they had different fathers. And it was the first time she had admitted the full extent of his father's abilities.

"So all this magic and sorcery stuff is true?" Gevan was so shocked at her admission about the magic that he almost missed the information that Lily was only a half-sister. "Wait –does Lily know any of this? We have different fathers?"

With tears gathering in her eyes, Vita stood up again and went to the window. Staring out, she said, "Not yet, but it seems it is time to talk to her as well."

Gevan stood and set the box on the table. He walked over to her and gave her a hug from behind. "I am sorry, Mother. I don't want to hurt either of you. We don't have to say anything, and I don't have to explore this any further."

Vita stepped out of his hug and turned to him, "No. I won't have that. I knew this day might come, and I have to own up to all this." Although her eyes were still full of tears, her voice was resolved. "If Strand has come to you, it must be important. These dreams you have been having are more than I hoped."

Gevan wiped the tears from his mother's eyes with his thumbs. He kissed her on the forehead. "Now what?"

"For tonight, take the box to your room. It is yours, and you will need to figure out how it opens. I will talk to Lily tonight while you are out to dinner with Harry. When you are back, we can talk more."

Gevan nodded silently. Vita walked over to the door, picked up her apron, and looked back at him. "I love you, son." Then she opened the door and went back to the kitchen.

Gevan stood there for what seemed an eternity, then took the box up to his room. He needed to get ready for dinner.

Chapter 7

Gevan and Harry were finishing up dinner. They had a seafood chowder Harry recommended and some nice wine. The conversation was light and easy, just filled with what they did over the day. Gevan didn't talk about the discovery he had today, though. There was still too much to find out.

As they were leaving, Harry asked if they could go and sit on bench across from the restaurant. It was the end of the street, two blocks west from where the bakery and boarding house was. It was small park with one oil street lamp and two benches on each side of it. The park was bordered on the two sides and back with waist-high bushes with a yellowish leaf.

"Thank you so much for dinner, it was very good," Gevan said as they walked across the street. He sat down on the bench on the right of the lamp. Harry stood in front of him for a minute.

"You're very welcome. I enjoy my time with you. It's been a short time, but I feel very close to you."

"I feel the same, Harry." He wanted to tell Harry everything going on, but wasn't sure if he would believe him or understand.

Harry sighed, then turned and looked the restaurant across the street. It was a simple front, with large windows. The two large wooden doors of the entrance stood open, and they could see people still at the tables eating, drinking, and laughing.

Harry turned back toward Gevan and stood there shifting his weight from one foot to the other. He seemed uncomfortable as Gevan watched him. Then sat down next to Gevan and held his right hand.

"Gevan, you remember I told you my father passed away recently?"

"Yes." Was Gevan's only reply.

"I also said I was up for a promotion; one I wasn't sure I wanted." Harry seemed to hesitate with each part of the conversation.

"I know. Where is this going?" Gevan could sense Harry's tension.

"I have to go home and resolve this. I didn't let my brother know I was leaving, and he has likely been trying to figure out where I am. I have been doing a lot of thinking while here, and we need to finalize what we are going to do."

"When are you leaving? How long will you be gone?" Gevan was getting nervous.

"I am leaving on a boat tomorrow evening back to Fraycia. I have to be there until this is decided." He turned to Gevan. "But I would like you to come with me."

Gevan was a bit surprised. He didn't know what to say. "I don't know if I can, I have my duties at the bakery. I have so much going on."

"You mentioned the man who was going to start helping you. Can he fill in while you are gone? I would really like you there when I complete this."

Harry looked at Gevan and stared directly into his.

"Harry this is much more than just the –" Gevan started.

"I am the oldest of the two twin princes, and I am to take the throne," Harry blurted out. "I am considering letting my brother have it instead. I could really use someone on my side when I go back to the palace tomorrow."

Speechless with shock, Gevan stared at him. "What?"

"When my father passed, I was next in line. I came here just to get my thoughts together. I wasn't sure I wanted to be king. I still am not sure what I want to do. I do know I have been away for too long and need to get home to talk to my brother."

"How was this not part of what you not told me this already? It's not a small detail. You're a royal." Gevan wasn't sure how to react.

"I am so sorry!" Harry said earnestly as he turned back to Gevan. "I didn't think I would meet someone, especially someone so special. Your friend Jack inviting me to join your group wasn't expected. I was going to lay low and just regroup." Harry sounded miserable.

Gevan was quiet for a moment. He didn't know what to think. He wasn't mad; he was confused. He had so much going on at home right now, but he also wanted to be there for Harry. How could he do it all? "What time is the boat?"

"It sails at sunset." Harry said as he raised his right eyebrow.

"I cannot say I will be there right now. I have to think, and I have to talk to my family. I wish I could just go, but I have responsibilities, commitments." Gevan wanted to go, he really did.

"I understand. Walk me back to the boarding house?" Gevan agreed and the two stood up and walked two blocks to the street and turned left to go up the block to the boarding house.

"If I don't see you tomorrow, I promise I will come back," Harry said. "I will send word when I am home and what is happening."

"You better." Gevan reached over and kissed him on the lips and held it for a long moment. "You better," he said again. Without another word, he turned and walked up the street toward home.

As he climbed the hill, he fought back the sadness. He couldn't look back to see if Harry was watching. Gevan needed to get home, talk to his mother, and look at the box from his father. There was so much racing through his mind.

∞∞∞

Lily and Minna were finishing up the dishes while Vita was ensuring the morning's deliveries were sorted and ready. Philip had come by and talked to her; she was happy to have some help for Gevan. He was going to start in the morning and go with Gevan on the deliveries.

Just as Vita was finishing up, there was a knock at the door. "Lily, will you get that?" she asked.

Lily walked over to the door and opened it. "Hi Jack. Come in."

"Thank you. How are you?" Jack asked as he entered the kitchen and noticed both Vita and another woman in the kitchen. She was slightly taller than the other two, with silky brown hair that was just longer than her shoulders, with both sides tucked behind her ears. When she turned to look at who was walking in, he saw her tanned skin and blue eyes. He was taken with her as soon as he saw her, even with the flour on her face from cooking.

"Hello, Jack. Gevan is still out to dinner with Harry," commented Vita as he walked into the kitchen. He walked past Vita to the sink and took Minna's left hand and kissed it as one would the hand of a royal.

"Hello ma'am, I am Jack. You are?" Jack smiled as he looked at her; she was blushing.

"This is Minna, she is working with us," Lily, looking puzzled, responded for her.

"Very nice to meet you, Minna." Jack let go of her hand and turned to Vita, "Is Gevan home?"

Everyone in the room laughed, and Jack looked at all of them, confused. Clearly he hadn't heard Vita earlier, or if he had, it didn't register. "What?" He asked.

"Nothing," replied Vita. "He is still at dinner with Harry. Would you like to wait and have something to drink until he's home?"

"If I am not intruding," Jack replied.

"Of course not. Why don't you go into the sitting room, and Minna will bring you a mug of ale if you like." Vita's mouth twitched as she suppressed a smile. She was sure he wouldn't mind.

"Of course, thank you." Jack turned and headed to the sitting room. Lily started to giggle.

"What was that?" asked Minna.

"That, my dear, was a smitten man," Vita said briskly. "Now get into the bathroom and freshen up while I pour this ale you are about to take to him." Vita pushed Minna toward the bathroom and turned to the sink to grab a mug. She pulled a mug of ale from the cooler to the left of the sink, poured it, and set it on the dining table.

"Lily, go and check on Minna," Vita suggested, but before she could, Minna returned from the bathroom. She had cleaned her face and removed her apron. She had a nice figure and was wearing a plain blue dress buttoned up the front with a cinched waist. "Now that is better. Here is the ale."

Minna took the mug and left to join Jack. Just as she left the room, the door opened and Gevan walked in.

"Shhhh." Lily said immediately, and Gevan stopped before he could close the door.

"What?" he asked in low voice.

"Minna is in the other room with Jack. He seemed very interested in her." Lily was slightly giddy.

"Come into the shop so we can talk." Vita led them into the front shop. The door led in behind a long counter with wooden shelves on the front of it to display baked goods.

Vita walked around the left of the counter to a close table. Lily was the last in and closed the door behind her. She asked Gevan to bring a chair from the other table and they all sat around the small table.

After sitting, Gevan asked, "So what is going on with Jack and Minna?"

"There will be enough time for that later," Vita said seriously. "We have other things to discuss." She looked at Lily. "Please let me finish before you ask any questions."

Lily looked concerned. "Sure. Are you okay?"

"Yes, but there are some things you should know, both of you." She looked at Gevan, then at Lily, and began.

"Lily, I met your father shortly after my twenty-first birthday. Your grandparents had passed, and I moved to Perrl. I was staying at a boarding house when I met your father, William." She paused. "He was called Will; that's why I named you Lily."

Vita glanced at Gevan and then again to Lily. "We fell in love so quickly, but his parents… let's say weren't happy with our relationship. We decided to get married anyway and started a home on the other side of the town."

Vita stared into the distance momentarily. "We still saw his parents sometimes, but it was not the best relationship until I became pregnant with you." She took Lily's hands in hers. "But then your father became ill. The healers didn't know what it was. I was seven months pregnant with you when he passed."

Lily started to say something, but Vita stopped her. "Let me continue. Your father's parents blamed me and wouldn't have anything to do with me after that. I had some money saved from my parents, and I survived until I gave birth to you. I sold the house we had purchased and moved here. I wasn't sure what I was going to do when I arrived, but my mother loved baking and taught me well. I saw this store and knew I would make it a home."

Vita took a deep breath before continuing. "When you were eight months old, another man entered my life. I wasn't sure I wanted to move on yet, but the attraction was more than I had ever felt. At first, I had horrible feelings of guilt, but then the love overwhelmed those. The short time we had was worth the pain I felt when he had to leave. And it left me with your brother."

Lily looked at Gevan and then at her mother, full of what could only be called confusion. "So, all this time ..." She couldn't finish.

"I am so sorry," Vita said, tears springing into her eyes. "But I thought it would be best to not complicate your lives. I planned to raise you two as brother as sister, and I never thought anything would come up that would make me tell you these things." Vita started to cry. "I love you both so much and it pains me to have lied to you. I didn't know how to tell you after you grew up having one father."

Gevan took put his hands over both of theirs. "We are still a family." He looked at Lily. "I am still your brother and love you both."

"You *knew*?" She asked, pulling her hands away.

"Lily," Vita interrupted sharply, "Gevan just found out today. This is why we must have this conversation." Vita looked at Gevan and nodded, indicating he should tell his sister what he knew.

Gevan told Lily everything he had discovered and talked about with his mother that morning. He told her about the dreams, Strand, and even the box.

After he finished, Lily stood up and walked to the counter, then turned and looked at them both. "This is all real?" she asked.

"Yes, sister. It is all real. I didn't believe it at first. I still don't know how to believe it all." Gevan stood and walked over to Lily and gave her a hug. "Are you okay?"

"I don't know. I just need to be alone." She pulled away and walked around the corner, leaving the shop and going to her room.

"Mother, are you okay?" Gevan looked back to her, as she was still crying at the table.

She wiped her tears with her apron, "I will be. We all will be. It will take time." She stood and brushed needlessly at the front of her dress. "We should go back and check on Minna and Jack."

"Wait, there is more I need to talk to you about concerning Harry."

∞∞∞

Gevan looked out his window at the palace. By the time he had finished talking to his mother, Jack had left and Minna was gathering her things to head home. He bade her goodnight, deciding not to ask her about her visit with Jack, and headed up to his room.

His mother was very receptive to what he told her about Harry, though she was concerned about him going away. It wasn't uncommon for a royal to have a relationship with someone not of royal blood, but this was different. They were of two different kingdoms. And Harry wasn't just a royal; he was supposed to be king. With what Gevan had just learned, it would be complicated.

Gevan turned and walked to the sink and turned on the hot water. He took a cup from under the sink, with a brush in it, and took a razor from the same shelf. He rinsed the brush and started to lather the soap in the cup. He soaped up under his chin, neck, and cheeks. He rinsed the razor and began shaving his cheeks to meet the beard line he was growing.

His red beard was getting thicker, and he planned on keeping it a while. He began trimming under his neck, but just as he was finishing the last bit, his right hand began to tingle, and he nicked himself right in the center of his neck. He put down the razor in the sink and grabbed a towel to wipe his face and neck. The towel had quite a bit of blood on it; the nick was deeper than he thought.

Turning as he held the towel under his chin, he and saw the box from his dad on the desk. The carved portion of the map was glowing. He slowly walked over to it and saw writing appearing on the front of the box. It was like he was watching it being carved.

He pulled out the chair and set the towel down on the floor next to him. He tilted the box toward him to read what was now carved into the box.

To Reveal What You Seek
You Must Use What Is Of Us Both

Gevan stared at the writing. It was glowing like the map on the top. "What is of us both," he said out loud. *What the hell does that mean*, he thought.

As he sat there thinking, a drop of blood from his neck fell on the desk in front of the box.

"What is of us both," he repeated as he looked at the blood. He took his three middle fingers on this right hand and rubbed them where he cut himself. Then he took those fingers and wiped them across the inscription.

The box began to vibrate. Startled, Gevan let go of it.

As the box fell back flat on the desk, another light began to come from it. But this time it went all the way around the outside center of the box. When it had traveled all the way around, there seemed to be a seam in the box.

Gaven stared at the box as the glowing subsided. He reached out, grabbed it on both ends, and pulled off the top. He set the lid behind the box and looked inside to see a note on a card. Under it was something wrapped in a silk cloth.

He picked up the note and read it. "This was

a gift to me from the Augur when I discovered my abilities. It helped me in the beginning to focus those abilities and learn to control them. Keep it close until the time comes you no longer need it, then return it to the Augur. Love, Your Father."

Gevan placed the note aside and opened the cloth to see what was inside.

Chapter 8

Philip showed up early to help load the cart for the morning delivery to the palace. He has been up to the palace, but never inside. He was both excited and nervous, especially after Gevan let him know he would be gone for a few days and Philip would be doing the deliveries as of the next day.

Gevan had risen early to write down the order of deliveries and a description of how they were sorted and marked. He spent some time walking Philip through the list in the kitchen before they began loading the cart.

"I think we have everything for the palace," Philip finally said, as they placed the last baskets on the cart.

Gevan reviewed what was in the cart and what was in the kitchen. "We do," he agreed. "Mother," he yelled in the back door, "we'll be back for the rest." He didn't wait for a response, but directed Philip to open the gate, climbed on the cart, and took the reins. Gevan shook them slightly so the horse began to pull the cart out; he paused after turning right on the street so Philip could climb on.

"You ready?" Gevan asked.

"If not, it's too late." They both laughed.

It was a short ride up to the palace. As they passed the pond on the left, Philip looked at the gates. The view was far more impressive than he imagined. He hadn't been this close before; it was unbelievable. The walls were easily fifty feet tall, and the yellow-brown stone seemed to sparkle in the sunlight. Philip could see the top had small windows the guards could look out and see for miles, as the palace sat on top of a hill at the base of the mountain.

"You with me, Philip?" Gevan could tell he was taking it all in.

"Yes, I have never been this close to see the sparkle in the stones. It is amazing."

"You've never come up here as a kid?" Gevan was surprised. "Most everybody does, at least to the pond."

"No, I didn't have a lot of friends growing up. I played around the boarding house and dock mostly." Philip had been shy growing up as an only child, and he had found it hard to make friends.

"Well then, you will be making a lot of new friends delivering the baked goods! People love getting sweets!" They both laughed.

As they reached the gate, Philip found him-self amazed all over again. Made of wood and two-thirds the height of the wall, the gates seemed over a foot thick. There was only one guard at the gate, but as they pulled through the entryway, they could see that the yard was full again of the guards practicing.

"What's going on here?" Philip asked.

"It's a long story," Gevan said, focusing on guiding the horse. "I will have to explain on our way back. This is why our delivery to the palace has been larger." Gevan didn't want to start the story until after he introduced Philip to Shorty, and they unloaded the baskets.

"If you look over there at the corner of the palace closest to us, that is the kitchen where we go deliver." Gevan pointed to where the path went up to the eastern corner of the palace.

Philip stared wide-eyed. The palace was made of the same stone the walls were, but the sheer size of it was overwhelming. It had to be four to five hundred feet wide and at least five to six times that in length. The height was three times that of the wall, four times in some places.

"Gather yourself, you will be seeing the palace every day. I still am amazed at it, but you will get used to it as well." Gevan wasn't totally honest. He was amazed every time he came in. He hoped to see more of it someday.

As they pulled up to the door, Gevan pulled the horse to a stop and climbed down. As Philip was getting down, Shorty came out of the kitchen. Gevan introduced the two and explained he would be gone for a few days and Philip would be doing the deliveries alone.

They unloaded the baskets and put the empty ones back on the cart. After saying their good-byes, they headed back down to the gate to get the rest of the deliveries loaded and ready for delivery.

On the way back, Gevan began telling Philip about the guards and the story he knew – but he didn't let Philip in on any of the other parts he had learned from Strand. He knew they were getting ready to fight something; he just didn't know what yet.

$$\infty \, \infty \, \infty$$

Strand was sitting on the couch close to the door. Avae was in bed resting. He contemplated their trip to the Augur a few days back and what Avae had learned. She was going back home today to take the message to the Elf Queen, and he wasn't sure if he should go with her.

Strand also knew he needed to revisit Gevan and find out what he had decided. If Gevan wouldn't help, Strand would have to find Colvin and hope he was up to helping out again. Colvin's son having potentially more abilities than he did was unusual – it happened only when two magicians had a child. But that wasn't the case this time, Vita did not have any known magical ability. Gevan was special.

Avae entered the room seemingly un-noticed by Strand, who remained staring at the blank wall deep in thought as she walked over to the sink and poured herself a cup of water from the jug. She turned and looked at him. He seemed to be in a trance.

"My love, are you all right?" she asked.

He turned his head quickly in her direction, surprised to see her standing at the sink. He hadn't heard her enter the room. As always, Strand was struck speechless by her beauty, mesmerised by her purple eyes and jet-black hair that draped down over her shoulders as she stood there in her seemingly see-through tan sleeping gown.

Strand finally caught up to his own thoughts. "I am sorry. I was just considering all we have learned, and what we have yet to do." He stood and walked over to her, trying to ignore the growing heaviness in his heart.

After he kissed Avae on the forehead, she asked, "Will you be returning with me to talk to my queen?"

"I think I will escort you there and give my regards. I will only be able to stay a day, and then I need to return to speak with Gevan."

She put her arms around Strand's waist and laid her head on his right shoulder. "I understand. We never get more than a few days together at times, and what seems like a life in between."

He wrapped her in his arms. "Why don't we

go back to bed and spend some more time to ensure we can bear that in-between a bit more."

She lifted her head and kissed him on his lips. She put her hands behind her back and took his hands in to her, leading him back to the bedroom.

∞∞∞

Gevan was finishing packing his bag in his room. He had finished the deliveries earlier with Philip and returned home.

Lily was still a bit quiet after last night, but she didn't seem as upset. Vita had spoken to her a little bit, but Lily just wanted to have some time to process everything.

Minna had been glowing all day; she was having a date tonight with Jack tonight. She moved around the kitchen as if there was a song only she could hear and her movements were the dance.

Gevan double-checked his bag to make sure he had everything, then cinched up the top. After he put the flap over, he tied it off and moved it from his bed over to the floor by the door where the ladder was.

He walked over to his desk and opened the box his father had left for him. He looked at the note, lifted it up, and pulled out the wrapped-up cloth. Gevan held it tightly in the palm of his right hand before putting it in the front pocket of his trousers. He needs to keep it close.

He closed the note up in the box and turned to the door. Opening it, he grabbed the sack and tossed it down to the kitchen floor. As he got on the ladder, he closed the door to his room and climbed down.

Lilly and his mom sat quietly at the table drinking a cup of coffee. It was odd to be so quiet in the kitchen. "Lily," Gevan started, "I know you are still hurting, but please take it easy on Mother."

"Gevan, let her be," his mother insisted.

"No, he's right," Lily said. "I don't want to be difficult. I know you have been through a lot raising us alone. I can't imagine the choices you've had to make. I just am still confused. I don't understand everything going on with Gevan." Looking at her mother, she said, "I still don't know how you did this all with everything you went through." Lily and her mom both started crying.

"See what you started," Lily teased Gevan.

Lily and Vita both stood up and walked over to Gevan and gave him a hug together. "Be careful," his mother said.

"I love you, brother." Lily kissed him on his cheek.

"I will. Thank you for holding down the fort and working with Philip. I will be home soon." He kissed them both on the forehead, picked up his bag, and walked to the door. As he opened the door, he looked back to them and smiled.

Gevan walked out and closed the door. Two rights and straight down the road to a new adventure, one that made him nervous.

∞ ∞ ∞

Avae stood with Strand in front of the same wall that had taken them to her first meeting with the Augur. The meeting had given her much to contemplate, and had provoked long discussions with Strand to understand, before she could return home to her queen to relay the warnings.

Strand took Avae's left hand and asked, "Are you ready, my dear?"

"Yes. We also need to make preparations for the worst case."

With that, Strand held up his staff with his left hand to the empty wall. As the spiral began to open up, they could see a path with unlit torches in the midst of tall trees. When the portal was large enough, they both stepped through into a dense forest. They were near the top of Red Lake Mountain, where the elves protected the lake above the cloud cover that hid the top from view. The magic that protected the mountain top wouldn't allow him to portal any closer to the village.

Strand had been here only one other time with Avae. It had been many decades ago, and the trees had grown taller since then. Now they were lush with dark green leaf, and the bark a smooth swirl of browns.

The path went up toward the elven village in one direction, and down in the other direction to disappear into the clouds. The tops of the trees were not visible, but the light from the sun shone through beams of warmth.

The dirt path was lined on both sides with fallen branches interwoven with flowering vines of small blue and yellow flowers to maintain the boundary. The borders seemed to move slowly up toward the village, as if the path itself was showing visitors which way to go.

Strand could feel the magic coming from the surrounding forest. He could see it in the trees; they seemed almost to breathe as they swayed in unison in the slight breeze coming from the clouds surrounding them to the top of the mountain.

Strand had spent a week here before, but had never left the village or the path to explore. As they began to walk, he wanted to study a tree up close, and decided to step off the left side of the path to approach it. Before Avae could warn him, he was thrown back on the path, landing flat on his back.

Avae ran over to him. "Are you all right, my love?" She knelt down and took his hands to help him to his feet.

Once he was on his feet, still shocked, he asked, "What was that? I felt magic all around, but I was not expecting that."

"We have placed a protection spell to ensure nobody wanders off the path without express permission and an elven escort. Our people have sworn to protect this forest and the lake it surrounds. It gives life to the whole continent. When the humans arrived, our arrangement with the Augur had specific conditions. The main one was that no human was to disturb these lands. What you experienced would kill any mortal."

He looked into Avae's purple eyes. "You could have warned me. Even the last time I was here you could have mentioned it."

"We were... busy the last time you were here," Avae said with a smile and slight blushing of the cheeks. "We should be on our way; my queen will be expecting us soon."

They walked up the path. It was a short walk to the village. As they came to what seemed the end of the path, they approached a wall of the same woven branches and flowers. Where the path met the wall, it opened up, forming an arch for them to walk under. The path continued under the arch into a larger clearing surrounded by the same tall trees.

"This is still an amazing place to be," Strand said, not to anyone but himself.

"Yes, it is. When I return from a trip it's like

seeing it for the first time all over," replied Avae.

The clearing was over three hundred feet wide, except for a larger tree in the center. It had a spiral stairway all around it, woven like the branches guarding the path. The railing also was made from the weaving branches, but flowers lined the outside of the stairs and the branches holding up the railing.

The stairs went up a good fifty feet until the tree seem to spread open. Here were the queen's living quarters and the courtyard to receive visitors. There was a wall and a platform woven from the twining branches of the trees. It was an entire village of living houses, stairs, and platforms, all made from the trees.

"These are all made from our magic, helping the trees grow into what we need," Avae told him. "Nothing is cut or damaged for us to live here."

"I remember you explaining this to me last time, but the use of the earthly magic is astounding."

Avae took his hand. "Let us go and speak to the queen."

As they walked across clearing you could see the clan children playing near the outskirts of the clearing, some parents watched. Some were tending to gardens and others ensured the paths were kept clean. Groups of elves were gathered on small landings at their homes in the trees.

They came to the large tree in the center

and began climbing the spiral stairs. Once they reached the top, Strand could see all the naturally made homes of the elves in the trees just below them. None were as high as the queen's.

At the top of the stairs was a simple reception area. Benches came out of the walls all around the circular reception area. To the left of the entrance was the living quarters of the queen, also simple from the outside. A tall elf stood on each side of the entrance to her quarters. Both had the same jet-black hair as Avae, although the one on the right had some grey around the temples. Their eyes were a dark orange, their skin as fair as hers. They both had slim toned bodies, with nothing but knee-length loincloths and royal blue silk bands across their chests, showing them to be guards of the queen.

"We need to remove our shoes," Avae told Strand. They both removed their shoes and placed them on their left. Avae wore shoes only when travelling outside of her village. The elves walked around barefoot when home. Shoes were never worn by visitors in the reception area, even if they did in the rest of the village. It was a sign of respect for their traditions.

"Wait here," Avae said. "I will go see if my queen is ready." She approached the guards and they nodded to her. Then the vines covering the entrance parted on their own to let her pass.

Inside it was not as simple as it seemed. There was a sitting room with overstuffed pillows of red and green silk on both sides of the room and a raised platform in the center with a silver platter for drinks and food to be served on. The flowering vines wove all around the inside of the walls. On the opposite side was another door leading to the sleeping quarters.

As the vines closed behind Avae, they opened to the sleeping quarters and Queen Fenrae walked through. "My queen," Avae said as she bowed slightly, "I hope the lands keep you well." It was the typical greeting of elves, because their magic both came from and protected the lands.

"Avae, my beautiful daughter, they do. I hope the lands keep you well," Queen Fenrae replied, then walked around the platform to her daughter and kissed her on the cheek. The queen was slightly shorter than her daughter, but had the same purple eyes and hair of jet black, with streaks of grey showing through.

"They do, Mother. I have travelled with Strand to visit the Augur. We have so much we must speak of."

"I hear you, my daughter. First, let's get some food, and then we will talk." The queen sat down on one of the pillows and indicated Avae should sit across from her. "Olvoc," the queen called.

The vines opened and the elf with the greying hair stepped through. "Yes, my queen?"

"Please have Tharla bring some food and wine. Ask Strand to join us."

"Right away." Olvoc bowed and left. The vines remained open and Strand walked in.

"Queen Fenrae, I hope the lands keep you well," Strand said as the vines closed behind him.

"They do. I hope you are well. Please sit with Avae. I understand there is much to discuss. We will have refreshments soon. Until then, why don't you catch me up on what you have been up to with yourself since we saw each other last." It was best to wait until after the food was brought and they were alone again to discuss news from the Augur.

Strand sat on the pillows next to Avae, then looked around the opulent yet comfortable chamber. Even though there were no windows, there seemed to be a slight yellow glow from the walls that lit up the inside of the room.

Strand spent a few minutes just talking, not about much, since it had been relatively quiet with the peace they had enjoyed for the last century. He had spent much of his time in the magicians' library on Bone Isle.

Tharla returned with a platter of fruits and vegetables, accompanied by another server bringing a pitcher of wine and some silver mugs. The two women set the mugs on the silver platter in the center of the room, poured three mugs of wine, gave each a cloth napkin, and left with a bow.

"Very well now, my daughter," the queen said, "what message did the Augur send you with?"

Avae began. "You remember the agreement that brought the humans to this land a century ago, and the reason for their need of escape. The same source of the destruction of their homeland is building strength to make a return. Its main target seems to be the Red Lake."

Queen Fenrae's eyes opened wide. She stood and picked up her mug of wine, and walked to the door to her sleeping quarters. Then she turned and looked at her daughter. "How is this possible? The protection around Old Fraycia after what happened there has shielded our lands from detection."

"It seems not all of the relic was destroyed, as once thought," Avae replied. "Those responsible weren't strong enough to detect or even make a move, but they have been feeding and getting stronger. The Augur cannot see yet where they will be able to enter our land, but it will happen within the year or sooner. As the time gets closer, we will be able to determine a more exact point of attack."

Strand added, "We have an opportunity to beat them once again, and hopefully for good. There is a young man, son of Colvin. He can be much stronger than his father. We will need his power if we are to survive this."

"This son of Colvin, where is he?" Queen Fenrae asked.

"He is in the Kingdom of Ethas. He knows he is needed. I will make a trip tomorrow to discuss

his training with him. His powers are just now beginning to show." Strand tried to sound confident
that Gevan would agree to help.

"What of his father, Colvin? Will he be of
any assistance?" The queen had met Colvin once,
at the time the agreement was made with the
Augur to bring the humans to their land.

"Mother, nobody has seen him in almost
twenty years," Avae said. "After he left Ethas, his
whereabouts have been unknown." Avae herself
had never met him, but she knew of him from
Strand.

The queen walked back over to her pillow
and sat down. Then she fixed her penetrating gaze
on Strand. "Tell me more of this young man and
his potential."

Strand began to tell her what he knew.

Gevan walked down to the dock where the
shipping officer had told him the departure would
be tonight. There weren't a lot of people around
for there to be a ship leaving dock; it was actually
pretty quiet. There were three ships docked. Two
were very large with four masts. Those two each
had one or two people on deck.

As he came to the end where he was told
to go, he saw the third ship, with three masts and

a deck swarming with people. It was very well kept, painted in bright green and gold. The name was *Serpent of the Sea.* The bow came to a point with an elaborate carved head and partial body of a sea monster, with eyes of a red stone and scales painted gold and silver. There was a fin down the center of the head that went all the way down the spine; it was painted red to match the eyes.

Just above the waterline was a row of eight windows, each with a glow of light coming from inside. As Gevan walked up to the ramp leading to the deck, he heard his name yelled from above. He looked up and saw Harry standing at the top of the ramp.

"Come aboard, Gevan!" Harry yelled down.

Gevan waved and paused for a moment. He looked at Harry. Was he sure he wanted to do this? His mother had assured him everything would be all right. Philip was helping out with the deliveries. But that all seemed trivial compared to what he was carrying in his right trouser pocket, and what it meant.

He took a big breath and walked up the ramp, holding on to the ropes. Suddenly he was nervous for a whole different reason – he had never been on a boat before. He had never been off of land.

He reached the top, and Harry gave him a hug and kiss on the cheek. "Welcome to *The Serpent.*"

"Whose boat is this?" Gevan was impressed

with the care taken to the embellishments engraved in the serpent, the deck railing that tied into the tail of the serpent, and the upward spiral carving on the masts. The deck was clean and smooth, but not so much to make it too slippery when wet. The carved serpent's tail continued onto the deck into a coiled position.

"It is our family boat. I sent word a few days ago to my brother to send it for my trip home. It arrived this morning." Harry motioned for a deck hand to take Gevan's bag and told him to take it to his quarters. "Would you like a tour?"

"Maybe later. Harry – is there somewhere we can be alone?"

"We can go to my quarters or the royal dining room."

"Food sounds good. Are you hungry?" Gevan was a bit nervous and wanted to sit and talk about what to expect when they arrived in Fraycia the next day.

"I am starved. I skipped lunch getting ready to leave. Follow me." Harry led him to the stern-side stairs under the main mast leading below deck.

When they reached the bottom, Gevan stopped in amazement. The walls were polished and shined. To the left of the stairs was a door opening into a hall next to the stairs; it led to the captain's quarters. The captain had stairs under the last mast, but this connected him to the royal quarters if he needed.

There were five doors, two on each side and one at the end of the hall opposite the stairs. "My quarters, well ours for this journey, is at the end of the hall." Harry pointed to the door.

"The door next on the left is the dining room, and this here is the kitchen. The door on the right of our quarters is a meeting room, and this door here is guest quarters." Harry took Gevan into the dining room.

Inside was a simple, yet elegant wood table that would seat eight. A servant's door to the right led into the kitchen. Two windows looked out to the other side of the dock. The wall opposite the kitchen entrance was a long table with candelabras on is. To the right of the door, the wall was covered with a tapestry that must be the family crest.

"Let's sit here, closest to the kitchen." Harry pulled out the first chair for Gevan. He then pulled out the chair next to him on his right and sat down. Gevan was surprised, as he had expected Harry to sit at the head of the table. "How are you doing?"

Gevan looked at Harry, then reached over and kissed him gently on the lips.

Chapter 9

*The time is soon. You must prepare for what
is coming, and I will help you.*

Gevan jumped awake and sat up in bed. The voice was still echoing in his mind. But it was becoming more comforting than dreadful now. It left him curious to discover who was speaking to him in his dreams. It was a relief to know he wasn't imagining the voice, even though knowing still left him confused on what to do.

Gevan thought it best to shake off the dream for now; he had forgotten where he was for a brief moment. He was in Harry's bed on the ship heading toward Fraycia.

It was the most comfortable bed he had ever slept in, and larger. It had a carved headboard of the same family crest on the tapestry in the dining room, and four spiral carved posts with silk material in the same green as the boat was painted.

The sheets were of fine, soft linen with a

gold silk comforter. There was a wooden bench at the foot covered in brown leather, and a night stand on each side of the bed. Feather-filled pillows made sleep come easily.

On the opposite wall was the door to the anteroom; on both sides of the bed were two more doors. To the right was large dresser, then a small table with two chairs by the window. On the opposite side of the room was a couch built into the corner of both walls. They were covered in wool, the same green as the bed cover, with a small table in front. There was another window next to the couch.

He turned to sit on the right side of the bed as Harry came out of the closer door, which led to a bathroom. "Good morning," Gevan said with a smile. They had eaten dinner and talked a little about what to expect when they arrived this morning. They had retired to the bedroom afterward.

"Good morning, handsome. Did you sleep well?" Harry stood there in nothing but a towel. His chest was covered in the same dark hair as his head. Gevan stared at the man he slept had next to the previous night.

"I did, thank you," replied Gevan. "I have misplaced my clothes, it seems." He stood up, letting the sheet fall back to the bed, and walked up to Harry, put his arms around his waist, and kissed him.

"They are folded on the bench at the end of

the bed. The maid took your shirt and undergarments to clean them. Your boots have been polished and are in the closet on the other side of the bed." Harry gave Gevan a playful slap on his bare butt. "Would you like some breakfast?"

"That would be wonderful. Coffee too." Gevan was not used to getting up without having to get ready right away for his delivery. "How long until we arrive?"

"We should be there in about an hour. Then the fun starts," Harry added with sarcasm as he walked around the bed to the closet. Opening it up, he pulled out two green silk robes. "Here you go, unless you want to show that off to the maid," he said, pointing below Gevan's waist.

Gevan blushed. "Not particularly." As he put the robe on, there was a knock at the door.

Harry took his towel off and tossed it on the bed, and hurriedly put his robe on. "Come in."

A young woman entered. She had blonde hair done in a bun and wore a white simple dress with a green apron trimmed in gold. She placed a tray with a pot of coffee, cream, sugar, and two cups on the table. "Shall I pour them for you, Sir?"

"That's not necessary. Can you bring us some breakfast? Thank you." Harry smiled as she left. He walked over to the table and poured coffee in the two cups. "Do you take it with sugar and cream?"

"Just black, thank you." Gevan walked over and sat down at the table with his back to the wall. Looking around the room, he asked, "One thing you never told me is why you don't want to be king."

Harry sighed as he set down the coffee pot. "I love my kingdom, my people and respect my traditions. I just cannot imagine having to be at the palace so much and not being able to travel. I want to go see the rest of the land." Harry sat down across from Gevan. "I want to find out more about the history of our people, more than what we can read."

"You don't think you can do that as king?" Gevan wasn't knowledgeable about Fraycia's customs.

"Not as much as I would like. Somebody needs to be there to make decisions and help rule. My brother Jon isn't as keen to travel." Harry always had been the more curious one.

"Wouldn't it make the king able to make more informed decisions if he has seen and experienced the world on his own?" Gevan asked. "You would expect his people, your people, to trust you more." Gevan poured more coffee in his cup. "Your brother doesn't want it either?"

Harry paused before answering. "He feels we should follow tradition and I should take the crown. His fiancée agrees with him, so I need someone on my side."

"I will support you, no matter what you decide." Gevan was about to say more, but there was another knock at the door.

"Come in," Harry announced. The maid brought in breakfast of rolls, scrambled eggs, and fruit.

"Will there be anything else, my Prince?" the maid asked. Harry declined, and she replied, "I will be back shortly with both of your clothes." She nodded and left.

Harry and Gevan began eating. The maid returned shortly with the clothes and set them on the bench. She made the bed and left quietly.

Then there was another knock at the door. Harry announced to enter; it was the captain's Chief Officer.

"Your Highness, we will be pulling into port shortly. I will have a purser down to get your bags after we dock." Harry thanked him and he left.

"Looks like we should get dressed," Gevan said as he stood up and walked into the bathroom to get cleaned up.

Harry sat there thinking about the night before. Gevan wasn't the first man he had dated, but he was the first one Harry would introduce to his family. There was something about Gevan; Harry wanted to spend all his time with Gevan. He made Harry smile, he was handsome, and somehow mysterious.

∞∞∞

After Avae and Strand finished breakfast, they walked across the large clearing leading to the tree that held Queen Fenrae's home. It was still astonishing to Strand how the trees would bend and grow to create the homes the elves lived in.

They had been up late discussing what Strand knew about Gevan, and what had been told to him and Avae by the Augur. Strand needed to bid farewell to the queen and go speak with Gevan about his decision.

Avae's home was directly across from her mother's and, though lower in the trees, was still higher than everyone else's. It was made the same as all the others, of trees and branches magically woven into a home.

As they reached the top of the stairs, Queen Fenrae exited her home and walked over to greet them at the top of the stairs. "Good morning, my daughter. Good morning to you as well, Strand."

"Good morning, Mother." Avae kissed her mother on her cheek.

"Good morning, Your Highness." Stand took her right hand and kissed it out of respect, not any protocol. "I hope you slept well."

Queen Fenrae's piercing gaze lingered on him. "When will you be taking your leave?"

"I must leave soon. I wanted to bid farewell

to you before I go." Strand wanted to meet Gevan as soon as possible this morning, when he knew they would have some privacy.

"May the land protect you on your journey." The queen smiled at Strand. "Daughter, please join me for a walk after you see Strand off."

"Of course, Mother." Avae kissed her mother on the cheek again, and with Strand headed back down the stairs. They would have to travel back to the end of the path where the cloud cover began to where the magic of the stone would allow him to portal.

Once they finally reached the end of the path they had arrived on, Strand turned to her. "My love, we will be together again soon. We have much to prepare for." He pulled her into a tight embrace, pulled back, and kissed her lips tenderly.

"I love you, Strand. May the land protect you on your journey." Avae paused, then added, "And return you safely to me."

Strand turned to the cloud cover and held up his staff toward it. The clouds began to spiral counter-clockwise and the portal began to form. As the spinning sped up, the portal grew until it was large enough to walk through. With a final glace back at the woman he loved, Strand stepped through.

The portal closed behind him. For a long time, Avae stood there, staring where the portal had been. Then she whispered, "A lot depends on you, my love."

∞∞∞

Strand stepped out of the portal and walked across the field toward the pond where he and Gevan had met the other day. He found the log they had sat on and took a seat, waiting for Gevan to come out of the gate after his morning delivery.

After a few minutes, Strand saw the cart exit the gate and head towards the pond. As it came closer, he saw it wasn't Gevan in the seat. He jumped up and darted to the road, right into the path of the cart and the horse.

Philip pulled the reins hard to stop the cart. "What are you doing in the middle of the road, old man?" he shouted.

"Old? You have no idea, boy!" Strand replied in jest. "Who are you? Where is Gevan?"

"Who are you, may I ask?" Philip wasn't sure what information to give out, and not sure what this short old man would want with Gevan.

Strand didn't reply. Instead he walked over to the right side of the horse until he was look-ing up at the boy from the ground. He stared into Philip's green eyes and got all the information he needed.

Strand was concerned with the unexpected turn of events. He had been to Fraycia only once, to help with the relocation from Old Fraycia with Colvin. He could portal there, but he wasn't sure how the landscape had changed in a hundred years.

He would have to take the chance and find a way to get to Gevan in the palace. He must see Gevan and begin his training. This new relationship could stand in the way of the young man's willingness to train with Strand. He needed to get back to Bone Isle to see if there was an updated map of Fraycia to see if he could portal to where he had been before.

"Carry on, Philip."

Philip looked around; he didn't remember stopping. He wasn't sure why he had parked in the middle of the road, but knew he needed to get going so the deliveries would be done. He started back down the road to reload at the bakery.

∞∞∞

Jack sat in a rather simple and empty room in the westernmost corner of the palace. It was where most of the planning was done for the guards. He was sitting in the center of three chairs to the right of the door. The three chairs on the left were empty.

Across from him was another door centered on the wall, with an empty dark wooden desk and chair on the right and two suits of armour on the left. They were older versions of what the guards wore now, but still maintained, with the look of having recently been polished. The wall to the right had a window that overlooked the south castle grounds; to the left was a map of Cruconia.

Jack had been asked to meet with the Royal Ambassador about his desire to join the guard in some capacity to help improve relations between the Three Kingdoms. His father, Tomas, had spoken to the Ambassador the day after Jack had brought up the idea. Jack didn't think he would be so nervous, but he was still excited.

He sat there deep in thought, so much so that he almost didn't hear the door he was staring at open. Tomis came out and closed the door behind him and asked, "Are you ready, son?"

"As ready as I will be, Father." He stood and Tomas put his hand on his shoulder.

"You will be fine, Jack. The Ambassador is receptive to the idea. It has been a while since he has had anyone take interest in politics as much as him." Tomis turned and walked toward the door, with Jack closely behind.

Entering the room, Jack was surprised at how different it was from the room he had just left. The Ambassador's office was not simple at all, although it wasn't elegant, either. The walls were covered with bookshelves from floor to ceiling, the two windows on the right being the only spaces not covered in books.

In the center of the room was a large desk, also covered in books and papers. A large, plush red desk chair sat behind the desk. The only other furniture in the room was the two couches facing each other with a long short table in the middle by the windows. Both were covered in the same red plush fabric as the desk chair, and arranged so one could look out the widows to the right.

The Ambassador was sitting on the couch facing the door. He was a middle-aged man, tall and slender, with dark brown hair greying at the temples. He wore a simple yet expensive-looking untied robe of deep green that ended at his knees. Underneath he wore a white shirt and brown leather trousers tucked into tall boots, though more formal looking than the guards' boots.

"Jack, this is Ambassador James Randell. Ambassador, my son Jack." Tomis' introductions were a formality, as each knew who they were meeting.

The Ambassador rose to greet Jack. "Good morning, son. Your father has told me many things about you."

"It's a pleasure to meet you, Sir." Jack shook the Ambassador's hand. "All these books, I could get lost in this room."

James and Tomis just laughed, which made Jack blush. The Ambassador patted him on the back. "Young man, I am glad you like all these books. If you're going to join me, you'll need to get to know what's in them. Some predate the century of peace we have now."

Jack looked from both the Ambassador to

his father and then back. "I would be honored to learn from you, Sir."

"For starters, call me James behind closed doors," directed James. " 'Ambassador' will suffice when we are in formal settings." He motioned them to sit on couches by the windows. "Your father has given me a background on the studies you did after primary schooling. What is the most interesting thing you learned?"

Sitting across from his father and James, Jack thought for a moment. He had always been interested in history and the relationships between kingdoms. After a moment, he began, "The distinct lack of relationship between our kingdoms, and the lack of clarity about what was behind the war all those years ago. No books I found went back far enough to indicate why the Three Kingdoms were fighting, or how the peace was brought. No treaty, no surrender, just an end."

James stood and walked over to the windows and looked out at the grounds. Without turning around, he said to Jack, "Young man, there is much not written about those times, and what is written is guarded with the highest security." He turned and looked at Jack. "How much you learn depends on how far you go."

Jack felt a sense of deep seriousness in the last comment. He stood and walked over to the Ambassador. "When can I begin, James?"

James looked at Tomis and then back at Jack. "First thing tomorrow. Now let me have some more time with your father."

"Of course, thank you!" Jack was nervous and excited. "I will see you at home, Father."

Jack turned and left the room. Tomis stood and walked over to James, and they both looked out over the grounds.

"James, thank you for allowing my son to work with you. You will let me know how things progress?" Tomis was sure his son would be eager to learn and do what needed to be done.

"He seems like a fine young man. If he is half the man you are, I think he will do fine. I just hope he is prepared for what he is going to learn." James knew the history of the war, the kingdoms and how it had all begun. The history was well documented, but also well concealed.

"I won't pretend to know everything, but with what I do know, I am confident Jack will handle it." Tomis was in a position to know the basics only, although he had learned more recently with his promotion.

"I have faith in you and your son." The Ambassador did not add that he was a close confidant of King Lewis, so he already knew of Strand's visit and warnings of what was to come.

Strand stood in the middle of an enormous

room full of books from floor to ceiling, which was easily twenty feet high. The room was lit by a glow that seemed to just be and had no origin, but was still bright enough to allow Strand to review all the maps of Fraycia on the large center table. Being only a century old, there weren't many accurate maps, as the town was always growing – as all of them were.

"There are no other books," came a voice from behind Strand. He turned, frustrated, and looked at the young lad up on the ladder. He was the assistant to the library keeper. In his late teens, he wore a simple pair of black wool pants and a long grey short-sleeved shirt tied with a golden cord.

"That's fine, Martin. These will have to do. I will need to study them a bit more to make sure I find a place not changed." Or at least Strand hoped he could find a place.

Martin climbed down the ladder and walked over to the table. He was the same height as Strand, with long blond hair and green eyes behind a pair of round glasses with wooden frames. "I will leave you be then, Sir. Please ring the bell if you need anything else." There was a bell by the door that was used to call for assistance with the books; the library's keeper was particular about keeping track of all the volumes he had been charged with. The new keeper had come about 10 years earlier, and it had been frustrating to Strand ever since; he liked being able to get what he needed on his own.

He looked at the three books on the table, then at the door. Strand asked himself, "What will he do, put me in the dungeon?" He gathered the books, took a hold of his staff, and pointed it in the air. He was going to study these in the comfort of his home.

<h1 style="text-align:center">Chapter 10</h1>

Gevan had been in Fraycia two days. The arrival had been uneventful. They had docked at the western Royal Docks next to the castle. The commercial docks were on the north shore of the island, so Gevan hadn't seen the city yet.

Upon arrival, they had been greeted by servants and taken to Harry's quarters. Gevan hadn't met Harry's brother yet, and had pretty much spent his time alone when Harry was in meetings with his brother.

The quarters surrounded a circular central courtyard with a small pool, trees, and a garden. The north side was a sitting room for entertaining, much too formal to lounge in. The eastern and western sides were both more casual, with the eastern side housing the dining area. The southern side was a large bedroom. Gevan hadn't thought there could be a more comfortable bed than what he slept in on the boat. He was wrong.

Sitting in the garden on a blanket, wearing a pair of tan shorts and sleeveless white shirt, both made of fine linen, Gevan was reading a book on Fraycia's history. He had found it on the desk in the formal receiving room.

"You must be the handsome lad I have heard so little about," came a female's voice from across the garden.

Looking up, Gevan saw a stunningly elegant woman. She had long blonde hair hanging loosely over her shoulders. As she walked toward him, he could see her figure under the knee-length fine linen dress that fitted her body perfectly. It had a tan under-lining with a lace overlay. She wore a pair of sandals that tied around her shapely ankles.

Gevan stood. "If I am, may I ask who you are, my lady?" He knew she must be of some importance by the way she was dressed.

She giggled. "I am Chell, Prince Jon's fiancée. You must be Gevan."

He took her hand and kissed it, as he felt he should. "It's a pleasure to meet you. I am Gevan." He looked up and was amazed at her purple-bluish eyes. He had never seen anything like them.

"No need for those formalities," she said as she kissed Gevan on the cheek. "If Harry has his way, we will be family in the future anyway." Shocked, Gevan didn't know what to say. "Let's sit back down," she continued easily, gracefully reclining on the blanket as Gevan joined her.

Gevan gazed at her. "You're the first person, besides the servants, I have seen since arriving here."

"My apologies," she began. "I was planning on meeting you yesterday to show you around. I was delayed in town with my mother. She lives on the far end and insisted we begin wedding plans. Tonight, we will all dine, and tomorrow I will show you around town."

Gevan smiled. "That sounds wonderful. What have Harry and his brother been in such long meetings about? Is deciding the succession so difficult?"

"Oh Gevan, you haven't been around royals much, have you?" Chell laughed melodiously. "They can make a pebble seem like a hundred-story tower." Then she giggled and added, "What has Harry told you?"

"Not much. He wasn't sure he wanted the throne, I know, but Jonathan wants him to have it to keep with tradition. I don't understand why he doesn't want it." Gevan didn't get much more than that from Harry when they talked about it. "I know they are going through a lot of their father's things."

"That they are. Jon wanted to wait until Harry returned to begin looking through every-thing." Chell stood up and Gevan followed. "I need to get some things done. I will see you this evening for dinner. It was good to finally meet you."

Gevan smiled. "You as well. I will see you tonight." Chell turned and left Harry's quarters. Gevan returned to sitting on the blanket and gazing at the surroundings, still amazed at where he was. He decided to lay down on the blanket and close his eyes.

As he lay there with his eyes closed, he ran through all that had been happening in the last weeks. Meeting Harry, discovering his abilities, and the strange man Strand. The dreams he had been having, though he was still unsure who it was, seemed to be getting more comforting. He slowly dozed off.

$$\infty\infty\infty$$

Strand had been studying the maps for the last few days. As he stood in the library on Bone Isle, he knew where he had to go on New Fraycia, and that it was time to get Gevan started on his training. He set the books down on the table and turned to open a portal to the north shore of the island; there was no settlements there and it should be safe to step out there.

Strand raised his staff and it began to swirl the air in front of him. As it began to open, he could see the sand of the shoreline. Once it was large enough, he walked through.

As he stepped out of the portal, he dropped about a foot. He was knee-deep in the sea off the beach. "Damn, just a few feet more." He walked through the surf to the beach as the portal closed behind him. "At least I didn't step foot-first into a wall."

Strand reached the shore and found a spot under a tree to sit and take his robe off and wring it out. He hung it on a branch to dry a bit and took off his sandals. He had a map inside the bag he carried; he took it out and began to study his surroundings. He was a few hours from the castle.

He would not have time to let his robe dry completely, but he could take a short break to have a snack before getting to Gevan.

∞∞∞

Gevan stood overlooking a man in a dark robe, kneeling by a well. The man slowly raised up and turned to look at him.

"Why are you here?" asked the man.

"I don't know," replied Gevan.

"Gevan, this is not your time. You need to stay away from Fraycia." The man's hood concealed his face.

"I don't understand," Gevan said as everything went dark. Gevan shot awake. He was being shaken by Harry.

"Are you ok, Gevan? You were talking quietly about a well or something." Harry was kneeling next to Gevan on the blanket.

"Just a dream. I am so glad to see you." He sat

up and gave Harry a kiss. He then rested his head on Harry's chest and asked, "How are the meetings going?"

"Good. Everything is resolved, but we need to talk before dinner tonight. First, I would like to take a bath and continue this conversation in bed." Harry gently pushed Gevan from his chest and gave him a smile and wink.

"Sounds perfect to me," Gevan responded. They stood and went to the bedroom, where the large tub had already been prepared by the servants. They both stripped off their clothes and climbed in, Harry first and then Gevan with his back to Harry's chest.

As Harry rubbed a bar of soap over Gevan's chest, soaping up his red hair, he asked, "How have you enjoyed your time here so far?"

"I haven't seen much. Chell did come by today. She seems very nice."

Harry chuckled. "She is very much as she seems. Jon has his hands full with her, but they complement each other." Harry reached on the table next to the tub and took a small cup, filled it with water, and rinsed off Gevan's chest. "I am sorry we haven't been out much. After dinner tonight, that will change."

Gevan sat up and turned around in the tub. "I am glad you have come to a resolution, and I do want to hear all about it." He paused. "But after we are done here." He leaned forward and began kissing Harry.

∞∞∞

Strand stood outside the servant's entrance of the castle, waiting for someone to come to the door. He decided he wanted to be as unnoticed as possible. The front of the castle seemed very busy this evening, and even though he could persuade others to forget seeing him, there were too many to take a chance.

The door opened and an older lady came through. She was dumping out a pot of water and almost threw it on Strand. "I am sorry, sir. What are you doing…"

Before she could finish, he reached into her mind and made her forget he was even there. It was like she didn't even see him. As he walked by her, he looked in the door and saw a guard; he wasn't looking his way and was preoccupied with one of the younger servant girls.

This was the laundry room; there were lines hung up with linens drying everywhere. It would be easy to sneak through unnoticed. As he was making his way through the linen to the entrance, he thought to himself, "What is it today with me and water?"

He reached the entrance and looked to make sure nobody noticed him. He opened the large wooden door. It creaked loudly; he paused and turned. The noise in the room had cloaked the sound of the door. He poked his head out and saw that the hall was empty. Strand pulled the door closed behind him; the creak seemed louder as it echoed in the hall.

The hall reached out in both directions; he was not sure which way to go now. He went left. "Why not?" he said in a low voice.

∞ ∞ ∞

Harry finished putting his boots on and turned to look at Gevan still sitting up on bed, with the sheet sitting just below his waist and his arms folded behind his head as he leaned back against the headboard. "I am going to regret this, I know, but I am heading to the kitchen to talk about preparations for dinner. I should stay here, though." He stood and walked around to the right side of the bed and gave Gevan a kiss on the lips. "I will be back shortly."

The kitchen was bustling, cleaning up after lunch and getting dinner ready. When Harry walked in, everyone got quiet and turned to him. "Please, carry on." Harry still was uncomfortable sometimes with how formal the staff was. He had grown up with a lot of the people who worked for the palace. Going from playing swords with sticks to becoming their king was going to be even more difficult than being their prince. He still needed to discuss this with Gevan.

"Your Highness," a voice came from behind the soon-to-be king.

Harry turned to see a slim, tall woman. She had grey hair in a bun on her head. She was the same height as him, wearing an ankle-length green dress tied with a gold waistband.

She had been in the kitchen since before Harry was born. His earliest memory was of her as head cook. She was always giving him and Jon cookies between meals, spoiling them. Since his mother had passed away when he was young, she was almost like a mother figure.

"Vessa, it's good to see you. I am sorry I haven't come by since I have been back," he said as he gave her a hug. Her name was Vanessa, but as a child he had been unable to say it, so he always said Vessa. It stuck as a nickname for him and Jon.

"It is great to see you as well, Sir." She was being formal in front of the staff; he had always insisted she call him Harry when they were alone. "Is this a social visit, or can I help you with something?" She was now the head of the kitchen, managing the staff and menus.

"Both, really. We need to talk about dinner tonight. It will be important, with just me, Jon, Chell, and Gevan. We will be discussing some confidential kingdom plans, and we will need discretion from any staff coming in and out." The four were going to be talking about the ceremony of his taking the crown and the role of Jon, but it was important for Chell and Gevan to be on board, and if they had any questions, to be able to ask them.

Vessa replied, "I will have everything set up and come and check on you myself during the dinner. I will ensure nobody disturbs you."

"If you have nobody you else you trust, I appreciate your help." Harry wasn't expecting Vessa to do it herself. "You have so much more to do."

"It will be my pleasure. And don't worry about me, I can get all my stuff done." Vessa cared about these two who were as close to children to her since she never had any of her own.

"Can we sit and talk about the menu? I have a few things I would like to make sure we have." Harry was going to try and have a few of Chell's and Gevan's favourite dishes.

They sat down at a small table, and she began to take notes as Harry gave instructions for dinner.

∞ ∞ ∞

Jon and Chell sat on a bench in the garden centered in his living area, which was identical to Harry's. The living areas were both designed by their mother when the twins were born. She didn't get to see them finished; she died before construction was complete. It was an addition to the castle and was connected by the main hall, but there was also a back hall between the two that only the builders knew about. The twins had used it as children to get back and forth in the night. Their father was going to have it removed from the plans but couldn't since their mother had designed it.

"You met Gevan?" Jon asked Chell.

"Yes, he seems very nice. He will need some instruction on the ways of the palace, but I think he will be up to it." Chell knew Harry would be taking the crown. It was what Jon wanted since Harry was the oldest, even if only by a few minutes.

"It will be the first time we have two male royals. Do you think the kingdom will be receptive?" Jon knew his brother had been attracted to men from an early age, but they had never really worried about heirs to the throne as children. Succession was one of the concerns Harry had about taking the throne.

"Yes, my love. We will lay out the succession plan and they will be fine." Chell knew that Jon was concerned about more than just this. Same-sex couples were common, but there were still pockets of people who didn't like it. History read that after the last war, it was seen as a responsibility of the sovereign to have children to help repopulate the kingdoms. So many seem to have been lost in the battles, though details were still vague.

Jon looked at Chell, knowing she was trying

to comfort him without bringing up the resistance. "You are correct, dear. I am going to return to the office and sort out some more of Father's papers before dinner. I will see you back here to get ready."

Chell kissed Jon on the right cheek, and then he rose and walked out of the garden. She sat there contemplating this evening's dinner and hoping all would go well. There were still a lot of people who would not be comfortable with a same-sex couple on the throne. It would be a challenge. One she hoped Gevan was ready for.

∞ ∞ ∞

Gevan was standing naked next to the bed and about to get dressed when he heard a voice from behind. "We have to be going, so you should get dressed, unless you plan on traveling naked across country."

Startled, Gevan grabbed the sheet from the bed and wrapped it around him as he turned to see the short old man standing in the doorway.

"Strand! What the hell are you doing here?" Gevan was surprised to see him. "And how did you get in here?" Which was a question he knew right after he asked it didn't really didn't need to be answered.

"We need to go, Gevan. We have much preparation to do before you will be ready to help fight off the threat that is coming." Strand stood there with his staff in hand, his voice and his face solemn.

"I can't go now. We have a dinner tonight, and it is very important to Harry. I know he will be taking the throne, and I don't know what that means for us, for my so-called destiny you have in mind for me."

"This destiny is much more than a dinner or a throne, it is life. It is preventing the destruction of the Three Kingdoms. The Augur has seen much, and unless you prepare, well, I don't know of another way." Strand walked over and sat on the bench at the end of the bed. "I fear it will be worse than the first time."

Gevan put his pants on and went and stood in front of Strand. "What do you mean by 'the first time'? You're so cryptic. You don't give me any information. There's so much hidden from our history."

"It's difficult to explain, but I can show you. We have to leave now, though." Strand stood and walked around Gevan to the floor on the right side of the bed. He picked up his shirt and tossed it to him. "You had best be getting dressed and gathering your things. Don't forget what your father left for you."

Gevan put his shirt on, pulling it over his head. "I told you I can't go right now, not tonight."

"You don't understand, boy! If you don't go

now, there may not be another chance." Strand had visited the Augur before returning the books to the library. He was at a critical path between two futures. One where Gevan left with him and began to understand what was coming, the other where he stayed to understand that Harry was to be king. If he stayed, he would feel too obligated to Harry to leave. Gevan would not be able to fight off the coming threat; he wouldn't understand his powers enough.

"What does that mean?" Gevan was getting frustrated and his voice was getting louder.

"You've been having dreams, right?" Strand knew about them; the Augur had told him Gevan had begun to connect to his father though his dreams.

"Yes, but what does that have to do with this?"

"Some of those dreams have included an unidentifiable man. Someone you have spoken to." Strand didn't want to go into too much detail about Gevan's father, but he needed him to understand what they were up against.

Gevan hesitantly responded, "Yes. A dark figure in a dark cloak. Why?"

"You are dreaming about your father. What is happening in this dream?"

Gevan sat down on the bed. "My father?" He was not sure what to think. "It's a man, kneeling by a well and then standing up. Both times I have dreamed it, he speaks to me as if I am there."

"He *sees* you in your dreams?" This was something Strand had not expected.

"Yes. he says I am not supposed to be there. Asking me why I am there, but I usually wake up right away. It's rainy, there are burning buildings and charred humans all around. It's disturbing. I couldn't even understand how something like that could happen." Gevan paused and then asked, "You're telling me it was my father?"

"Yes, I believe so. And by the description, I know where you are going in your dreams." Strand walked over and stood in front of Gevan. "And when."

Chapter 11

Jack had been riding with the battalion of soldiers for three days now. The Ambassador thought it would be good for him to go on the training mission with them. It would give him some good field experience for travelling between the kingdoms. They were heading west toward Windrip, about a week's ride from Ethas.

They were stopping for the night to make camp. Jack and the two dozen soldiers each had their duty assigned to them. Jack had been assigned to scout the surroundings, reporting any sources of water and gathering wood for the campfire.

They were at the base of some small break-off streams of the Windrip River. It was another four days up the river, according the map, until they would reach their destination in Windrip.

They stopped in a large clearing of trees, only about five minutes from the stream. Jack reached the bank and sat down, setting the water jugs next to him. It was peaceful, the most peace he had felt since joining the palace as an understudy to the Ambassador. Though he was quite enjoying this adventure, the peace outweighed hearing two dozen men debating the purpose of this mission or complaining about their asses hurting.

He noticed the stream water was quite clear and cool. He got onto his knees and began filling the jugs. He threw some over his shoulders and carried the remaining in his hands. As he walked back to the camp, he again reveled in the peace of the woods. They were quieter than he would have expected.

Jack returned to the campsite and saw some of the tents were already going up. There were seven tents in total, placed in a circle. He was in the main tent with the two officers; the two cooks had a tent for them and the supplies, while the other five housed four men each. Each of the four men in the tent would take shifts guarding the campsite throughout the night.

He distributed the water and then went back out to gather wood for the fire. It wasn't difficult to find enough wood; there were fallen branches everywhere. He made several trips to gather enough wood for the night and the cooks.

By the time he was done, everything was set up and the cooks were had begun cooking the evening meal. It was during this time he typically met with the captain and lieutenant to review the day's events and plan for the next day. It was a formality really; if there was a battle, it would be more of a strategy meeting than sitting back with some ale and deciding who was going to be complaining most the next day. The most official conversation they usually had was which route to take the next day.

The evening went by uneventfully and they were called for dinner. It was usually some wild game found in the area. A couple of the men would head off while camp was being built to hunt and clean the evening meal, with enough left over to have for lunch the next day on the road. Breakfast was usually some bread and spiced grain dish.

Tonight was different. The hunters had come back empty-handed, not finding any game they could cook up. So the cooks had made a stew from some leftovers and vegetables they had in the wagon. Jack got his food and sat down near the fire, listening to hear who would start the evening grumbling.

Harry returned to his quarters and called out for Gevan, but there was no response. He walked into the bedroom, deciding to wake him up. He had left him in bed when he went to the kitchen, but had run into Jon on his way to his father's office – soon to be Harry's office.

He had joined Jon for almost two hours to

go over some more of the papers. There was a lot to go through, so many journals they had found. Many were from previous generations, ones they never knew existed. It could take years to go through them all and categorize them.

As he walked into the bedroom, he saw that the bed was made and Gevan wasn't there. He walked across the courtyard, around the garden to the meeting room. It was also empty. Just as he was about to go check out the dining area, a page came from the western sitting room.

"Your Highness, Master Gevan asked me to give this to you when you returned." The boy handed Harry an envelope. He was quite young, with blond hair and brown eyes, wearing light green trousers and a white shirt tied with a green woven belt around the waist.

"Thank you, lad. When did he give this to you?"

"About two hours ago, Your Highness." He seemed nervous. It was obvious he was new; he couldn't have been more than fifteen.

"Thank you, you may go." The boy turned and left out the main door next to the meeting room. Harry opened the envelope and read the letter inside:

Harry,

There is so much we have experienced in a short time, yet there is so much we don't know about each other. Much you don't know about me, things I am just learning.

I have to return home immediately, and I wish I could explain, but in a letter it's just not possible. You probably wouldn't believe me anyway. I will return, I promise.

I am sorry about dinner. I know you will be King soon; you will be amazing. I hope to be back for the coronation.

I will send word as soon as I can. I love you.

> *Yours,*
> *Gevan*

Confused, Harry walked into the bedroom and saw Gevan had taken his things. He didn't know what to think. He wasn't mad. But he was heartbroken. And he was worried. He needed Gevan by his side tonight.

He walked over to the sitting room. This was where he was able to lounge inside if weather didn't permit time in the garden or pool. It had a few couches in green velvet around the three walls and a circular wooden table in the middle with four chairs. The seats and back were covered in gold velvet. Immediately to the right of the door was a bookshelf next to one the of couches. It was a simple wooden bookshelf with all the books he had read as a child, and some portraits in frames.

The center shelf had a portrait of his

mother. He walked over and looked at it. She had been so beautiful, with long red hair and the bluest eyes. But he barely remembered her.

He rarely touched this portrait anymore. He picked it up, and with his other hand he found behind it on the back of the bookshelf a simple heart carved into the wood. It was put there in memory of her. He rubbed his fingers on the heart; he hadn't touched it in years. Then he pushed it. The bookshelf rolled back into the wall and turned to open the passage between the two brother's quarters. He pressed the heart again, replaced the portrait, stepping back into the passage as the bookshelf returned to its original position.

He walked down the corridor to his brother's quarters. He was visibly upset and didn't want to take the chance of seeing any palace staff. He had decided dinner wouldn't happen tonight; he was going after Gevan. He needed to know what was wrong.

Gevan and Strand stood near the western bank of a river. They had gone through one of Strand's portals from the palace to this place. He wasn't sure where he was.

"What are we doing here?" Gevan had told

Harry he was going home, but he knew they were going somewhere else. He couldn't explain to Harry that he was a sorcerer. Well, that he had the ability to become one. Strand had convinced him that he needed to see the place in person, the place he had visited his father in his dreams.

"This isn't where I was in my dreams," Gevan said. He was still a bit frustrated, but the chance to understand his dream was too much to pass on.

"This is as far as I can take us by magic. The place we are going to is protected by one of the most powerful spells your father ever cast. It keeps all life away. If any mortal was to get closer, they would wake up days later not knowing where they had been." Strand paused, then added, "No person was ever meant to step foot on that land again."

"How do we get there then?" asked Gevan.

"We walk. It's about a day away. We should make camp here tonight and start fresh in the morning. We will reach it by tomorrow evening."

Gevan wasn't happy, but he decided to take the magician's advice. They made a small fire and rolled out some blankets to sleep on later. Strand pulled some meats and bread rolled in a cloth from his bag and sat by the fire.

"Let me tell you a bit more about where we are going. Among those that know the history, it is called Old Fraycia."

Gevan looked up across the fire at Strand.

"What?" was all he could say.

Strand settled into his story. "Before we came to this land there were once four kingdoms in a much larger land. The two you know now, Ethas and Abareth, and the kingdoms of Charpet and Skooth. There was peace and an alliance between them all.

"The threat coming is not new, but we thought we had escaped and isolated it to our old land. All the survivors created one kingdom. That kingdom was Fraycia. It was a new start for everyone, so we thought.

"Then the so-called war a century ago split the kingdom into the three you know today. It wasn't a war, but an invasion which caused the differences in people to split once again."

Gevan listened to Strand tell the story and wanted to ask questions, but his mind was spinning just listening.

Strand continued, "What you will see tomorrow is the result of that conflict. It will be much easier to explain once there, but the spell your father put around Old Fraycia was meant to protect this land from the same invasion again."

So much of it was hard to believe and terrifying. He was beginning to understand what had happened, but still only begun to understand what was needed to stop it again.

"That is why these woods are so quiet. No living being can stand the effect of the magic your father cast. This is where the magic trails off; just on the other side of this river, about half a day's walk, it returns to normal. Even the seas around the center of the spell deter creatures from venturing into the perimeter of the spell." Strand eyed Gevan. "I am sure you feel a slight vibration in your bones."

Gevan hadn't really paid attention to it; he was too busy listening to Strand. "Now that you mention it, I do. I hadn't thought about it before. It's how I felt when I held the gift from my father."

"Speaking of which, you should wear it now. It is time for you to understand how it works." Strand watched as Gevan took the folded cloth from his trouser pocket.

"I haven't put it on yet," Gevan said as he handed the folded cloth to Strand. "I wasn't even sure what it would do if I did."

Strand put the small bundle on his lap and unfolded the cloth. It was an amulet of what seemed to be a claw. It held a deep green stone and attached to a heavy silver chain.

"It comes from the same place my purple stone comes from, the Augur," explained Strand. "There are many like it, of different colours. Each has a different ability given to it by the Augur.

"With the help of this one your father was able to fight the invasion as we brought over all the survivors from the continent halfway across this world we live on. It allows the bearer to focus their magic. There will come a day you won't need it, but until that day comes, you should never take it off."

Gevan picked it up and placed it around his neck. It hung in the middle of his chest.

Suddenly a strong sensation came over him and everything around him seemed to stop, even Strand. It was like everything froze.

Suddenly he heard the voice he had heard only in his dreams: *You are my ward and I your protector. I will give my life for you if need be, as I swore to do for your father.* Then everything returned to normal.

"What was that?" Gevan was both amazed and in shock. He had never heard the voice so clearly before.

"You felt something when you put it on? It was a centering of your powers." Strand was seemingly unaware of the freezing of time around Gevan.

"No," Gevan exclaimed, "everything just froze. Nothing was moving. I heard the voice I have been hearing for so long in my dreams."

"Ah, your guardian. You will meet him when it is time." Strand gazed into the fire. "All I know is that he is an immortal being and appears to each person differently. I never met him when he was with your father, but he was very fond of him."

Gevan felt different, yet comforted. "We should turn in; I want to get an early start tomorrow."

They both laid down into their bedrolls and

looked up at the stars. It was a clear night that seemed destined to lead into a day of uncertainty.

∞ ∞ ∞

Jack lay on his cot in the tent, listening to the silence. He could hear the crackling of the large fire in the center of the tents, and the men circling the camp on guard. Then it hit him. It was *too* quiet. There were no birds making noises during the day; he hadn't seen any tree animals. There weren't even any fish in the stream. It seemed so odd, but it could be normal for this part of the land.

As he tried to drift off to sleep, he was thinking of Minna. He had gone on a few dates with her and felt things he hadn't before. He couldn't wait to get back to her.

Chapter 12

Vita and Lily were finishing up cleaning after the morning delivery had left for the palace. Philip had been doing a great job in Gevan's absence, but they missed him. Minna had gone to Jack's to see if his mother had heard anything from him.

There was a knock at the kitchen door. Lily yelled, "Come in!" She expected it be Minna, but why she was knocking was unknown. Lily turned and began, "Minna, why – " She stopped. It was Harry.

Vita turned when her daughter stopped speaking. "Harry! What are you doing here?" She said in concerned tone. "Where is Gevan?" Before Harry could answer, she continued, "Forgive my rudeness. Please come in; it's good to see you. I am just surprised to see you and not Gevan."

"It's good to see both of you as well, but now I am confused too." Harry had thought Gevan was home. "I received a letter yesterday saying he was coming home, and it seemed urgent. But none of the boats seemed to have a record of him leaving.

So I brought my boat overnight to see if every-thing was ok."

Vita's face turned white. "He has not re-turned here. If he came back on a boat, he hasn't made it home yet." She walked over to the table and pulled out a chair. "Please sit," she said to Harry. "Lily, get us some coffee and sweet rolls." She sat down with Harry. "What did the letter say?"

Harry handed her the letter. She read it and set it down on the table. "I think I know where he is," she said after a moment, choosing her words carefully. "Or rather who he is with." Vita knew he was with Strand. She knew what was happening, that he had started to hone his craft.

"Who?" Harry asked, concerned.

"First, there is much you need to know. It isn't my place to tell you, but you have come a long way and I cannot let you leave without knowing the truth."

Lily brought coffee and rolls to the table and sat down with them. Vita began to tell Harry about Gevan's father, Strand, and the gifts Gevan had recently been made aware of.

∞∞∞

Gevan and Strand had been walking for a few hours. As the time passed, and the sun rose higher in the sky, they could feel the buzzing of the magic more and more with each step toward the center of the spell. Gevan understood now. The center of the spell was the well where he saw his father in his dream. Stand hadn't explained the fire and destruction yet, but he said it would become clear when they arrived.

"How much farther until we get to the town?" Gevan was asking both in anticipation and out of fear. He wanted to discover the truth, but at the same time he didn't want to know.

Looking ahead into the distance, Strand responded, "We are almost there. When we get to the edge of the city, we will need to go through an illusion spell. I can get us through, but once inside I don't know what to expect."

"What do we do when we get there? Are we staying? I thought you were going to help me understand this amulet and how it will work." Gevan still didn't know what he was capable of, and in reality, neither did Strand.

"This is just a fact-finding mission," began Strand. "You will know what you are up against and then we will return to Bone Isle. There we can begin exploring your powers."

They walked a little while more, but suddenly Gevan felt ill. "I don't feel so good," he told Strand.

"Me either, which is why we are here." Strand knew they were about to enter Old Fraycia.

They both stopped and Strand asked Gevan

to stay back. He took a few steps forward, lifted up his staff, and closed his eyes. Gevan felt an energy begin to flow from the old mage; then he saw a ray of light shoot from the purple orb in Strand's staff. It didn't swirl like Gevan was used to, but it began a rippling effect a few feet in front of them. It was as if he threw a stone into a lake.

In the middle of the ripple, a hole began to form, through which he could see the ruins of a town. The town was familiar to him. It was the same one that was in the dream. The hole kept getting larger, until it was big enough to walk through.

"Let's go, we don't have much time to get through before it will close again." Stand directed them through the hole of the illusion, and it closed behind them.

The town was still black from fire and there were piles of charred wood where buildings once had stood. The bodies were no longer standing; over time they had settled into piles of ash in the streets. It was eerily silent and like walking through a graveyard, only the bodies weren't buried. There was no new growth. No trees, grass, or bushes. Everything was still dead.

"This is worse than I imagined from my dreams," Gevan stated grimly as he took in the sight. They began to walk down the broad street, passing bones of adults and some children. Nobody had taken the time to even bury the dead. He didn't understand. "What happened here?"

As they entered the town square, they came to the well where he had seen his father in his dreams. This was the center of the spell; he could feel an immense wave of energy flowing from the well.

"This is where it began and ended," Strand said. "I told you the story of starting a new life and the relic that your father found. But what I didn't tell you is that the relic is what brought this destruction. Your father destroyed the relic to keep the intruders out." Strand's gaze swept across the square, his voice remaining strangely calm as he described the horrific events. "The destruction caused an explosion of energy and fire, killing and burning everything within the city."

"My father did this!" It was an exclamation more than a question. "WHY?" Gevan's voice cracked with strain. "Why did he do this with all these people? How could he kill them all?"

"It's more complicated than that, Gevan." Strand's voice was emotionless. "He would have saved everyone if he had the choice. This is why he had disappeared for so long. His guilt forced him into self-imposed exile. He only came back to go and talk to the then-king of Ethas. Only when he met your mother did he feel he had a chance again. But even that couldn't fix him."

"I don't understand." Gevan was conflicted between the man he didn't even know being a great sorcerer he was told helped so many, and what seemed like a man who murdered so many.

"Fraycia was settled here about twenty years before this ... *event* happened. They were attacked by demons from the depths of another realm. Demons of great power, and even greater hunger for human flesh."

"Demons?" Gevan was even more confused now. "You didn't mention anything about this last night. Another realm? All of this really exists?"

"This and much more than you can imagine. You will get to know all about it as time goes on." Strand went on. "The demons began to scorch the earth and torment and devour humans and any living being they could. It gave them more power.

"Your father discovered the ancient relic that had allowed them to come to our realm. It was an idol held by an order of priests in the Kingdom of Charpet. The Order of Marpa protected the Idol of Marpa, which kept the demons in their realm. If the idol was destroyed, they would roam free in our land.

"Your father discovered it had been damaged during an earthquake, cracked. The Order of Marpa hadn't had time to discover and fix it before the demons began coming. The idol acted as a sort of beacon for them to come to. They sent a few sentries through and destroyed the idol, allowing legions of demons to begin their journey."

"How did everyone end up here?" Even though it seemed like a fantasy, Gevan was beginning to be frightened.

Strand continued. "By the time your father

discovered how it happened, it was too late. Everyone was fleeing to the original coastal Kingdom of Ethas; they planned on sailing away. It seemed the demons couldn't survive without land and living flesh, so the water was the best option. Before they could leave, though, demons arrived and destroyed all the ships.

"Your father convinced the Augur to help the survivors escape to this land, where the Three Kingdoms are now. The elves were here, and it was a land with enough resources for our people to survive.

"That was when we were given these stones. Mine was to help open a portal to this land, and your father's was to help focus his abilities in closing the opening between the realms and destroying the remaining demons."

"So, you two brought all the survivors here?" Gevan asked. "Then how did this happen, if he destroyed the opening and the demons?"

"There were just a handful of survivors from Charpet. They escaped to this new land during the initial invasion, but what nobody knew is they brought the head of the idol with them. They thought they could remake it and once again ensure the demons were locked away.

"For twenty years they secretly lived in Fraycia and worked on a way. It was a small piece of the idol, but it worked like a beacon still. It took a while for the demons to regroup and find it, but they did. That's when they came again, but only a few and your father came to help."

Gevan began to ask another question, but before he could get anything out, a large blast of energy threw him and Strand to the ground. As they sat up, both a bit stunned, they saw a figure in the sky.

"Run!" Strand yelled at top of his voice. "This way!"

Even though he was a man over two centuries old, Strand moved quickly. Gevan followed him and they ducked into a still-standing building.

Once inside, out of breath, Gevan asked, "What was that and where did it come from?"

Strand stared out the door of the building, searching the sky for the creature. "I am afraid of what it is, and even more afraid of where it came from. I won't know until I see it again for sure, but I think it was a demon."

"A demon! How? If my dad destroyed the rest of the relic, they can't come here."

"I don't know." Strand said, then pointed in the sky. "There it is." They both looked up. It was a black figure that wasn't solid, but wasn't a shadow. It was something in between. Its eyes glowed deep orange.

"It hasn't seen us again, but it won't be long," Strand said tersely. "You need to create an energy ball to destroy it."

"Me? How?" Gevan had never done any magic yet.

"There's not a lot of time. You have to think in your head. Imagine the hottest heat possible. Cup your hands together. Visualize it, *see* it growing inside the protection of your hands."

Gevan cupped his hands, closed his eyes, and thought of the fire from last night at its brightest. He opened his eyes, but nothing was happening.

"Boy, you have to concentrate," Strand demanded.

"This thing out there wants to eat us, and you want me to concentrate on my hands?" Gevan was both serious and sarcastic at the same time.

"Either you do or next time you see that thing, one of us is its meal. The more it eats, the stronger it gets." Strand looked out the door to see that the creature was coming towards them. "It's spotted us!"

Gevan moved toward the door and closed his eyes again. He cupped his hands and then imaged the light again. But not the fire; that wasn't strong enough. Something else, something brighter. Gevan imagined he was holding the sun in the palm of his hands.

Suddenly a light began to grow in his cupped hands. Gevan felt a tingle in his hands and opened his eyes. There, in his hands, he saw a red and orange ball that seemed to be a liquid fire. He looked into the sky and saw the creature approaching fast. He pulled his hands to his chest and threw the ball into the sky.

The fireball struck the creature squarely. The flying thing screeched in pain and plummeted to the ground. Seconds later it exploded into a bright light.

Gevan was frozen in shock and horror. After a moment, Strand said, "That was amazing and timely." He patted Gevan on the shoulder. "Now let's get out of here before any more come."

Gevan stared at him. "What if there are more? How do we keep them from escaping?"

"I have feeling I now understand the spell your father cast." Strand paused to think. "There is a reason why no living creature can come near here. I fear he couldn't fully close the way between our two realms. He had to keep everything away, but also them in."

As they began to leave the building Gevan asked, "Did I destroy that creature?"

All Strand could say was, "I hope so."

They made their way to where they could open the protective shield and leave Old Fraycia. They had a to walk back to the river to be able to use enough magic to portal to Bone Isle.

∞∞∞

Jack was walking to the river to get some water. They had stopped for lunch and were getting ready to move on to where they would make camp for the night.

He had noticed shortly before stopping that he was seeing birds and tree animals again. It was still peaceful, but more… *alive*, somehow. And the sounds of nature were preferable to the sound of complaining soldiers.

He reached the river bank and saw schools of fish swimming around in the middle of the water. Jack put down all the travel jugs he was going to fill with water and kneeled down next to a small pool of clear water. He filled the jugs one by one.

Jack sat there, imagining being here with Minna and how peaceful it would be to live outside the city. Away from all the hurrying around during the day, the sounds of drunk people in the streets at night, and all the horses and carriages on the roads.

After a few seconds of simply sitting in quiet and calm, he looked down into the pool he had just filled the jugs in. A fish had somehow been swept into the pool and was trapped. He stared at the fish, watching it swim around trying to find a way out. Then, in one lightning-quick scoop of his hand, Jack reach in and grabbed the fish. Without thinking, he took a huge bite out of the back of the fish. With a big smile, he chewed the live flesh and swallowed.

Chapter 13

Ta lay dazed on the ground. Ta was not quite sure what happened, but knew it hurt. The bright light flying toward it, the initial blow, the drop and then the agonizing pain of smashing into the ground. It had been sent here to survey for anything living and food. It was not prepared to fight.

Ta felt so weak. It was already difficult to keep any little form it had after coming out of the hole, but then those two creatures attacked it. It was able to get up, but there was no form to it. Ta couldn't see itself but could feel itself. It needed food, or it was going to die.

It saw the creatures that attacked it hurrying off. Ta decided to follow. After a few minutes, the shorter one was pointing a stick in the air, and a hole opened to another world. Ta thought there must be food there, something to eat. It hurried to follow the creatures through the hole, barely making it through before the portal closed closed behind the short man.

It was so weak, there seemed to be nothing

around to eat. The creatures stopped and sat on some rocks. Ta was afraid to get too close; they might hurt him again. If it was to report back home, it needed to eat and gain enough strength.

Ta suddenly took notice of the tall things around it. They were colourful, moving back and forth slightly. There were shorter ones around it too. These had little red balls on them. Ta reach over with what seemed to be an invisible hand and took one of the red balls. It felt life inside of it, an energy that was appetizing. Ta tossed it into its mouth and swallowed.

There was a bit of relief. It took a few more, and then a handful. Ta could feel the energy returning, but only a little. It needed something with more substance, with more life. There was no change to its appearance; it still was basically invisible, but it seemed to have a bit more energy.

It had almost forgotten about the creatures, Ta looked over and saw they had begun to walk again. It hurried to catch up. It followed them for what seemed like forever. It wasn't sure about time here; days could have passed. Maybe it was due to it being hungry. It saw a few of the red bulbs again and grabbed a handful as it walked by. They helped.

Later the creatures stopped again. Ta watched from behind a rock, and saw more of the red balls. It broke off two bunches and ate them as it watched the humans talking. Then the short man held up his stick again and the air seemed to begin to swirl. They were going to another world. How did they do this?

Ta ate all the berries, but knew it needed to follow them. It took some more berries and ate them. It felt enough energy to get to the hole quickly. The taller creature was stepping through; it needed to hurry. Ta jumped on the rock and pro-pelled itself forward as fast as it could. Then it realized it was able to fly again.

Ta picked up speed, but just as it was about to reach the hole, it closed. Still flying through the air, Ta had picked up so much speed trying to get to the hole, it couldn't slow down. It sped past where the humans had been, through some of the tall living creatures, over some moving liquid – and then suddenly, like hitting a wall, it stopped. Everything went dark for a minute.

After a few minutes, Ta slowly could see. Its sight was different. It didn't see energy sources; the colours were more distinct. It looked down and saw its hands were different. No claws, but five fingers. What had happened to it?

Suddenly it noticed movement and looked down to see something flashing through the water. It was alive, it was food. It took its new hand and grabbed it as quick as it could. Ta took a big bite of the creature, smiled, and swallowed the live flesh.

Ta was surprised at the flavor; it had never tasted anything like this. There were so many new sensations it was experiencing. Ta took another bite of the wriggling, slippery creature, and then another, until all that was left was some of the bones. It couldn't chew them for some reason. Ta tossed them in the lake.

As the energy of the food fed Ta, it began to realize it had taken refuge inside another creature. It had heard this was possible, but had never known another of its kind that had done so. Ta didn't have a long memory, though; it had been around only for a short time before being sent through the hole into this world. It had to find a way back to report what it had found.

Suddenly Ta felt tired; it needed to rest. It had been attacked, followed the creatures that attacked it, and then ended up inside this creature. It decided to close its eyes and then search for more food later. Ta would find its way back to the hole home after some sleep. It laid down on the ground and closed its eyes.

Jack woke up. He was surprised he had fallen asleep. He sat up and then realized he had a truly awful, foul taste in his mouth. He picked up one of the jugs and rinsed out his mouth and spat out the water, then took a drink. Fish; it was the taste of fish. But he hadn't eaten any fish. He rinsed his mouth and spit again.

Leaning over the pool of water, he dipped the jug in to refill it. He stood and picked up the bunch of jugs and started walking towards the camp. He didn't feel well; that was probably the reason he had the awful fishy taste in his mouth. Jack didn't even remember falling asleep.

He returned to the the men who were waiting for the water jugs. Everything had been cleaned up and the men were mounted, except for the lieutenant.

"Mr. Smark! We were about to send men after you," announced Lieutenant Persy. He was a young man, just a few years older than Jack. He stood a few inches taller than Jack, but wasn't as muscular. Persy was athletic, with dark hair, green eyes, and clean-shaven. He was wearing plain brown leather trousers, a tan shirt and brown vest, which was what all the men on the training mission were wearing. The only different item of Persy's uniform was the silver braided ribbon on his left shoulder identifying his rank.

Confused, Jack looked at the lieutenant. "What do you mean?" He still felt queasy.

"You've been gone for almost an hour," stated Persy.

Jack didn't realize it had been so long. He knew he had fallen asleep, but he certainly didn't want to tell that to the other men. It was better to claim to have been sick; after all, he really was feeling unwell. "I am sorry, I came down with some stomach issues and was sick. I lost track of time."

"You're feeling better, I hope," the lieuten-ant said as he mounted his horse. "Let's get mov-ing," he said to the others.

"I am, thank you." Jack walked over to his horse and mounted. He still didn't feel good, and he couldn't believe he had fallen asleep by the river for over half an hour. He guided his horse into the double line of riders as they headed out of the clearing. They had half a day's ride to the next stop for the night.

∞∞∞

Strand and Gevan stepped through the portal and it closed behind them. They were standing in a small room with a couch on the left and kitchen area on the right. Across from them were two doors, with one far on the left next to the couch.

Gevan looked around and asked, "Where are we?"

"In my house," replied Strand.

"You live on Bone Isle?"

"No, this is an unsettled part of the land. North of us is the Yellow Mist Forest," explained Strand. "The Elves of the Mist are pretty secretive, so nobody can travel past the forest."

Ever curious, Gevan asked, "How did you

find this place, then?"

"I was introduced to them many decades ago. They allowed me to pass through. I built this home here as a refuge and a place of seclusion." Strand paused. "I wanted to gather a few things before we head to Bone Isle, but now I think we should just stay the night here. We can eat and rest, and get a fresh start in the morning."

Gevan sat down on the couch. "Sounds good to me. This traveling by portal is very convenient."

"Yes, it is. It has helped out many times since we came to this continent. It has its limitations, though. Like not being able to portal too close to Old Fraycia. Most magic spells distort its focus, so when I go to the elves in the mountain, I have to walk up to there." Strand turned to the kitchen. "Would you like some ale?"

"Yes, please." Then Gavan asked, "I want to know more about the mountain elves. You mean the Red Mountain?"

"Yes. Why?" responded Strand.

"Nobody has ever gone up there and returned. Everyone thinks they all die or are eaten by animals."

Strand laughed harder than he had ever remembered. "No, boy. The elves live up there, protecting the lake. They have a spell that protects the mountain top and where they live."

"What is it like? Do they live in caves, or huts, or tents? Or have they built homes like us?"

Gevan was so curious; he had never realized there were elves. "What do they look like? Are they short?"

"Whoa, so many questions!" Strand laughed. "They are civilized, but their homes are...hard to explain. Someday you will likely meet them, or at least one of them." Strand was thinking of Avae. He wished he could go to her now. They had so much keeping them apart, and now this new coming fight.

Strand continued, "I need to sleep. And so do you," he added as he saw Gevan stifling a yawn. "You can have the couch. I will get you a blanket and pillow."

"Thank you, you will have to tell me more tomorrow." Gevan took off his boots and trousers.

Strand went into the bedroom and returned with a blanket and pillow. "Sleep well. We will get an early start. There is much to learn."

∞∞∞

Harry was still at Gevan's home with Lily and Vita. Vita had told him everything she knew about what had happened over the last few months.

"How is this all real?" Harry asked her.

"There is much more in the world than we all know," Vita replied, gazing pensively into her glass of wine. "Gevan isn't aware of what he will be able to do, but I understand his father was quite the sorcerer. After the war, magic wasn't really spoken of or used. Over the generations it just became a myth to everyone." Vita reached over and took Harry's hand. "It doesn't change who he is, or what he feels for you."

Harry gazed at her. "Oh, I never even considered that. It just makes sense now. He has been a bit guarded about some things. And his sudden disappearance without being on a ship." Harry thought for a moment. "Where would Strand have taken him?"

"There is only one place he can go and learn all he needs to know to become who he capable of being." Vita paused; it was place she had never imagined one of her children going to. "Bone Isle, off the west coast near the Ash Barrens. It's almost two weeks' ride from here to the coast."

All three of them were silent for a moment. Bone Isle was a place of legend and mystery; nobody knew what was really on it. There was no known way to get on the island. The cliffs were too high, and there was no known port able to land ships. Rumours were abundant about people trying to scale the cliffs and disappearing into a mist, not to return.

Harry was hesitant. Having lived his whole life by the sea, he had grown up with sailor's stories about Bone Isle. It was difficult to even think about the place without feeling a sense of wonder, awe – and yes, fear. But if Gevan had the courage to go there, then so could Harry.

"I can take my boat around the coast," he said finally. "We can dock on the island." Harry stood up. "I need to find Gevan. I will leave in the morning."

Vita looked up at him with a gentle smile. "You will need to be careful. Give the southwest coast a wide berth, or you may not find your way. The island is secluded. There is no dock, and the surrounding waters are full of large rocks. They… don't like uninvited guests." Vita stood up and gave Harry a hug. "Good luck. You are a good man."

Harry nodded to Lily without a word. She gave him a distant but warm smile before he turned and walked out the door.

After he was gone, Lily asked her mother, "How do you know so much about Bone Isle? And what did you mean about the southern coast?"

Vita sat down and turned to Lily thoughtfully. She wanted to answer her daughter's questions, but she didn't want to share too much just now.

"Gevan's father told me some stories. The coastal area isn't safe, from what he said." Vita knew there was a spell around an area there to keep people away. She didn't know the full extent of what happened; Colvin wouldn't talk about it, and she had never pressed him. She thought that over time he would open up more, but the time they had was short. It was only years later she discovered that whatever had happened was the reason he had left.

"What do you think will happen?" Lily asked, interrupting her mother's thoughts.

Vita took Lily's hand as she had Harry's. "I don't know, dear. Harry… he's on a mission of love. He doesn't know about the threat Gevan spoke of; I couldn't even begin to explain that. I don't even understand it myself." She sighed anxiously. "He will find Gevan, or he will not. If he does, he is being pulled into something none of us are ready for. If he doesn't, he will be heartbroken. That might be safer for him, though."

Vita stood resolutely. "All we can do now is get ready for tomorrow's orders. When is Minna coming back?" Vita carried two wineglasses over to the kitchen sink and set them down. Then she stopped and put her hand on the countertop. She began crying.

Lily walked up behind her and wrapped her arms around Vita's waist. "I am worried too, Mother. But Gevan is a stubborn and strong young man. He will be fine."

Vita turned to her daughter and took her hands, trying to smile through her tears. "After I lost your father, you were all I had. I didn't want to find love again; I wasn't even looking. When Colvin walked into my shop, it was… well, it was magical."

She reached into her apron and took out a hanky to wipe her eyes. "I had a second chance at love. Which didn't last long at all. He left and I was alone again. After a while, I found out I was pregnant." She shrugged her shoulders helplessly. "I wasn't sure how I was going to be a mother again and run this shop. I did it, though. I made a home for you and Gevan. And the thought of losing him in this mess… it scares me."

Lily gave her mother a hug. She was scared, too. Neither of them knew what to expect from Gevan's future. Or their own.

∞∞∞

Harry returned to his boat and set the crew to preparing to set sail. His crew had restocked for the trip back to Fraycia, but were sent off to gather more supplies for the new destination.

While he was waiting, Harry sat in the dining room writing a note to his brother Jon, explaining that he would be gone for a while, but didn't know how long. They had been planning to hold the coronation in just over a month, to coincide with the annual Festival of Elidi, a traditional summer festival that also happened to coincide with the anniversary of Fraycia's founding on this island.

There was a knock on the door. "Come in," Harry announced absently, intent on the letter.

The ship's captain entered, a middle-aged

man with grey hair and a beard that reached the middle of his chest. He was wearing the green leather trousers all the sailors wore, but where the crew all worked in tan shirts and brown vests, the captain's shirt was white, and he wore a gold vest.

"We are ready to push off, Your Highness. Is everything set?"

"I just need this letter given to the dock sentry to have it sent to my brother." Jimmy folded the paper and put it in an envelope. He took a stick of green sealing wax and held it over a candle on the table. When the wax was soft, he pushed it onto the fold of the envelope. Using the ring on his right hand, he pressed the seal of Fraycia into the soft wax. "Captain Grange, direct them to send this on the next boat to Fraycia. As fast as possible."

Grange took the envelope. "Yes, Your Highness."

Harry pushed his chair back from the table. "Then let's push off. We have a long trip and I want to get there as soon as we can." He stood and followed the captain out of the dining room to the corridor that ran almost the full length of the ship. The captain went right to go down the hall to take the envelope up to the deck, and Harry went in the door to the left, to his room.

Harry began to get ready for bed, his mind racing. There was so much going on right now, so many new responsibilities he was going to face. He got undressed and into bed. He wasn't sure why he was going after Gevan. All he could do now was wait to reach Bone Isle.

Chapter 14

Gevan was standing on a cliff overlooking a rough sea. It was dark, and only the sound of waves crashing on rocks could be heard. Next to him stood a dark figure. The only thing Gevan knew was that he was male. They didn't speak.

Gevan was conflicted. He knew somehow that he needed to save this mysterious figure. But at the same time Gevan felt an overpowering urge to destroy him.

He turned to look at the figure on his right; the man turned his head toward Gevan in return. Then his eyes flared bright orange and he suddenly lunged at Gevan.

Gevan shot up on the couch, his feet tangled and thrashing in the sheets. These dreams were so real; he was still panicking, and his heart was pounding.

Strand was at the kitchen sink; when he heard Gevan stir, he turned. "Are you all right, boy?"

"Yes, just a dream." Gevan's voice was a little shaky. "These damned dreams seem so real at times. And mostly they don't make any sense." Gevan sat up and put his face in his hands. "It's just like the voice I hear at times."

"Well, we should be going. I have gathered some things we will need." The old sorcerer indicated two traveling bags on the small dining table. "We will be staying at the castle a while. There is plenty of room there, both in and out of the castle. It's the only building on the island." Strand walked back into his bedroom.

Gevan stood up and put on his pants, then sat back down to put on his boots. He had lost track of how many days it had been since he left home. He missed his mother and sister. He hoped Philip was doing a good job for the bakery and everyone was well. With Strand's staff, they should be able to go see them. He would ask the old mage after they get settled at the castle.

Gevan stood, still a little groggy, and walked over to the sink, where Strand had left a pot of coffee. Gevan poured himself a cup and turned to lean against the sink as he drank. He began to think of Harry. He hoped the prince understood and wasn't too hurt. Gevan didn't want to leave, but knowing what he knew now, he didn't have a choice. He had been thrown into this new world and new war just because of who he was.

He was so lost in his sleepy and dream-scattered thoughts that he didn't notice when Strand came out of the bedroom. The old sorcerer stood for a moment, quietly watching Gevan. "Are you ready?" he finally asked.

Startled, Gevan downed the rest of his coffee. "As much as I will be." His picked up his bag from the dining table, and took his jacket off the hook where it was hanging by the front door.

Strand picked up his bag and staff. Gevan joined him by the wall as the mage began opening the portal to go to Bone Isle. As soon as it was large enough, Strand walked through and Gevan followed.

Gevan stepped out of the portal into a dark cavern with a large fire in the center of it. Strand wasn't anywhere to be seen. He couldn't have gotten far. Gevan wondered why they seemed to be under the castle. "Strand? Where are you?" Gevan called out, but he didn't answer.

"Strand isn't here, Gevan. I brought you here so we could meet." It was a voice in his head, but not like the one in his dreams.

Gevan was scared. "Who are you? What do you want?"

"No need to be scared, young man. I am friend, not foe." This time the voice was not in his head, but spoken aloud. It was calm and feminine, but not like one he had heard before.

"Then why don't you show yourself? You are hiding in the dark." Gevan stood in place and spun around to see if there was any sign of anybody.

"Very well," she said. From across the cavern, beyond the fire and where the light touched the cavern walls, a creature began to emerge.

It was the largest creature he had ever seen.

Gevan took a few steps back without even realizing it, until his back bumped against the wall of the cave.

As she continued to emerge, it became clear: she was a dragon. A *dragon*. Yet another children's story he hadn't believed was real. But this one was different. She was...beautiful. Her face was slim and elegant looking, her lizard-like body smooth and lithe. Her emerald-green scales had a slight shimmer to them; they almost seemed to glow in the light of the fire. Her giant, mesmerizing eyes were golden, and her chest had pearly-white scales that faded into the green.

As the magnificent creature came out into the light, she raised her stately head on its long neck. Gevan could see in the center of her chest a circle of gems, seemingly embedded into the shimmering white scales. Five gems sparkled: orange citrine, deep amber yellow, blood-red ruby, coal-black, and pearl-white. There appeared to be three gemstones missing.

The dragon gazed serenely down at him. "I am called the Augur," she introduced herself. "I felt it was time we met." Her voice was smooth and melodious.

Strand had told Gevan about his visits to the Augur and how she was the one who told him about Gevan. He had so many questions… too many questions. He hardly knew where to begin.

"How did I get here? I was going through Strand's portal."

"There are a great many things you will learn about magic, and you will master much in the near future. There are many things you will learn about me as well." She seemed to sit, folding her legs under her. She hadn't fully emerged out of the shadows. Although she was three stories tall, there was no indication yet how long she was.

"The powers of the stones are given by me," the Augur continued. "You can see on my chest the missing ones, one of which you wear around your neck, and another in the old man's staff." The Augur paused. "I can embody the powers of the stones myself, which allowed me to redirect you to me here."

"Strand will worry, how will he know?"

"The old man will be fine." The Augur finished laying down on her front legs. She eyed him piercingly. "I knew your father. He came to me a long time ago to help with the evacuation of the old land. I helped him work with the elves to migrate to the settlers to new land you are in now."

"I have heard so many things about my father." Gevan looked down, unable to meet her gaze. "Then I find out at Old Fraycia he was responsible for that destruction and those dead people."

The dragon sighed. "He is haunted by those deaths, Gevan. But the effect of your father sealing the last piece of the relic into the well and destroying it, weaving closed the rip between realms, was not his fault."

She shifted, her neck weaving back and forth slightly. "When he cast the spell to destroy the relic, the demons had already been able to break the tie to it. The relic no longer protected our world from theirs. The burst of energy your father unleashed struck at the same time the demons were able to rip away from the confines of the binding spell. It was the power of those two energies hitting the relic at the same time that caused such destruction." The Augur sounded almost sad. "It was not something anyone could ever have foreseen."

Gevan began to understand. "So that's why he put the spell around the city, to keep the chance of any demons away. We were there, and there is no life anywhere close. Everything inside the illusion spell is charred and dead."

"Except the small demon you encountered." The Augur had seen this was going to happen; she also knew they had not killed it. "You made a great attempt with your first spell to attack it. But...." She hesitated. "It wasn't destroyed."

Gevan was surprised. And, he admitted to himself, a little disappointed. "Well, at least it has nothing to feed on. It will have to return to where it came from or die."

"Things are not always as we think they

are," the dragon said sagely. "The demon didn't die, but it also didn't stay inside the protected area. It was able to follow you out of through the same hole you and Strand exited."

"What? We didn't see it." Gevan was worried now. "I have to go back. Can you send me back?"

"I am afraid it is too late now; it is gaining strength, and you will need to be stronger to defeat it. Stronger both in your abilities and emotions." The Augur knew the demon had possessed Jack, and she knew it would be difficult for Gevan to do what was needed when the time came.

"What do you mean?" Gevan was actually getting mad now. "Every day something new happens. I either have to give up something, or I find out one more way that I am not who I thought I was, or I'm hearing voices in my dreams. And the dreams, they are getting more real-feeling and frequent." He turned away and started pacing, trying to control his rising anger. "Is there anything else? Any other surprises? Sometimes I just want to walk away, take my family and let what happens happen."

The Augur sighed. "I have been around for centuries. I have seen many I know and care for live and die; I will see more in my life. It isn't easy, but being who we are, it is a part of our existence. We learn to understand it better, but I wouldn't say we get used to it."

Gevan sat on the floor of the cavern. "I just

don't know if I am up to this."

"The voice you hear will be a companion, a protector and a great help. You are not alone in this." The Augur's golden eyes remained on him. "He has been with your father since he was a child. There is more you should know, something only your father knows."

"I think I should be happy I am sitting down." It was sarcasm, but close to the mark of how Gevan felt.

The Augur laughed, a musical laugh that couldn't help but lift his heart a little. "I haven't laughed in while," she said, still smiling. Then she became serious again. "This is what you need to know, young man. Listen. Your father is not of this world. Therefore, you also have another connection besides Cruconia."

Gevan stood up and turned away from the Augur, his mind reeling. "What do you mean? Am I – are you saying – I am not of this world either?" His shook his head in wonder. "I mean I get it conceptually, but I cannot wrap my head around this. We are," Gevan paused, "aliens?"

"Of a sort." The Augur answered. "Your father was sent here when he was seven years old. His life was in danger on his home world, so to protect him, his mother sent him here. My abilities don't reach beyond our world, but this is what I was able to get from your father's mind."

Gevan thought for a minute. He moved over closer to the Augur. "I...don't really know what to think. What do I do with this information?" He looked up at her, an unspoken plea on his face. "Why did you tell me this?"

"It's part of who you are, who you will need to embrace if you are to be open to learning." The Augur chose her words carefully to ensure she was giving Gevan the correct message. "You were not born to this world. You don't have the limitations that those native to this world do. The world you come from is very similar, but the magicians there are of greater power than the ones here."

The Augur spent a short time explaining to him what she knew of the world his father came from – which wasn't a lot.

At the young age his father came to this world, he didn't have a good understanding of what was happening on his home world. The Augur had not been able to read much useful information from Colvin's young mind. Gevan listened and asked a few questions, but there wasn't much he could really learn.

Gevan stood before the Augur, studying her. He was thinking of what he had just learned while he stared at the gemstones on her chest. "Something just occurred to me," he said after a moment. "I have the green stone and Strand has the purple one. Who has the third one missing? What color is it?"

"That is a story for another time." The Augur seemed uncomfortable at the question.

"What do each of them do?" Gevan asked.

This was something the Augur didn't mind sharing. "They all stem from powers I have. You know of two; Strand's allows travel, while yours gathers and focuses power. The citrine has the power of fire, allowing control and use of its force. The ruby helps control the forces of the earth, much like the magic of the elves on the Red Mountain. And the amber, it helps harness the powers of the weather, as do the elves who live in the Yellow Mist Forest."

Gevan asked, "And the black and white?"

The Augur lowered her head closer to Gevan's, her golden eyes squinting as she looked at him. "Death and life," she answered simply. At that moment he was reminded powerfully that the Augur was...not human. Something in her voice and the directness of her gaze was chilling.

Then she pulled her head back. "Now it's time for you to join Strand. You have much to learn."

He instantly knew not to press any more on the gems.

"One more thing," the Augur added. "I did say I have seen many I know and care about live and die. You may live a long life – centuries, possibly. You must come to terms with loss. You cannot let it deter you from doing what is necessary. Though at times that will be very difficult." The dragon looked around distractedly, her thoughts clearly moving on to other things. "Now go. We will see each other again."

With that a portal appeared behind Gevan. It wasn't like when Strand used the stone, and the portal swirled from a small hole to a large one. It just appeared in full.

Gevan gave one last look at the Augur and stepped through.

∞∞∞

Harry had been awake for a while. He had eaten breakfast, read some documents he had brought with him, and paced the deck in the morning light. He stood by the main mast looking at the sea all around him. They could barely see the land off the starboard side as they made their way around the continent. This land wasn't a large continent, so sailing was expected to take three days maximum with good weather.

"Captain, where are we?" Harry shouted up to the quarterdeck where the captain was standing at the ship's wheel.

"About this time tomorrow we will be turning north as planned, as long as the weather holds," answered the captain.

"I am heading below. Keep me informed of any changes." Harry walked down the stairs to his quarters. As he reached to door at the end of the hall, he reflected on what Vita had told him about Gevan and his abilities. It still felt like all this was children's stories and not real. Shaking his head, he opened the door and went into his quarters.

Harry sat on the edge of the bed, then laid down. He finally realized why he was going after Gevan. Harry wanted him to know he wasn't going to push him away and he could do what he needed to, with his support. Harry didn't know what Gevan would discover, but he knew he wanted him in his life.

His thoughts began to wander back to the coronation. Harry had finally agreed with Jon that it was right for him to take the throne. Jon would succeed him if something was to happen; then it would go down the line of Jon's children – when he and Chell had them.

The challenge, if Gevan and Harry stayed together, was what Gevan's role should be. Harry was sure he wouldn't want to be Queen Gevan. Harry chuckled out loud. The thought of asking Gevan to be his queen… Harry could just imagine the look on Gevan's face.

There was no precedent for this in the history of Fraycia. Jon was home working on it with the royal advisors, just in case. They had known each other for only a short time, and being together was looking more as if it wouldn't happen before the coronation, but it was best to have it prepared if they needed it in the future.

He was hopeful they would be together.

$$\infty\,\infty\,\infty$$

Gevan stepped out of the portal to see Strand in front of him. The portal closed behind. In front of them he saw the castle. It was made of gray stone, unlike the others he had seen. It had a tall pillar on each of the four corners, and a large domed center. The corners each had a point at the top that seemed to have a slight blue glow emanating from it.

Strand looked back at the young sorcerer behind him. "I wanted you to see it from the outside before we went in. It's a sight, plain from the outside, but a sight none the less." He pointed to the top of the towers. "You see that glow there?"

Gevan had noticed it right away. "Yes."

"That is our warning spell. If anyone not invited approaches, the points glow red and a barrier forms around the castle." Actually, it had never been used, and it seemed to Strand useless until now, but it wasn't his decision to make. "I don't get why they ever put it in place, but we may need it in the coming months."

"I am sorry you had to wait here for me." Gevan indicated behind him where the portal had closed.

The old sorcerer was still intent on the castle. "What are you talking about, boy?"

"You had to be waiting here at least an hour

or more for me to come through the portal."

Strand turned and eyed him sharply. "You came out right after I did. There was no waiting." He stepped closer to Gevan. "What happened?"

Gevan turned and looked at the surroundings, not really looking for anything. He just felt a bit confused. "When I walked into the portal, I stepped out into a cavern and... I met the Augur. She said she redirected me there to talk. But if I came out right after you, then I must have imagined that. Maybe it was another dream from last night?"

Strand walked over to the confused lad and put an arm around his shoulders, resting his hand on Gevan's right shoulder. He started walking, gently directing Gevan with him to the entrance of the castle.

"The Augur has the ability to... you might say... distort time a bit," Strand explained. "She has six other stones on her chest. Each has a power, and that is what the sapphire blue one can do."

"I saw the stones. She described them all to me. All the but the sapphire one." Gevan stopped and looked at Strand. "It was missing."

Strand's eyes opened wide. "Did she say where it was?"

"No," answered Gevan. "She just said it was a story for another time."

Strand turned and started walking again, and Gevan followed. They didn't speak the rest of the way to the castle doors.

∞∞∞

Harry had fallen asleep while thinking about his coronation. He was awakened by a sudden jolt in the boat. At the same time there was a knock on the door. "Enter," he said loudly, sitting up on the bed.

One of the deck hands came in, a young kid who looked to be no more than seventeen. He was wearing the normal uniform but was barefoot. The blond, green-eyed lad said in a hurried voice, "Your Highness, the Captain asked for you to come up to the deck quickly." He turned and ran away before Harry had the chance to excuse him.

Harry jumped out of bed and ran out the door, down the hall and up the stairs. As he came out on the deck, he instantly knew why he had been summoned.

He went up to the helm and joined the captain at the wheel. "What is going on here?" Harry asked.

"I don't know, Sir. Suddenly the wind died, and the water got very calm. It was like we passed a line, and everything changed." The captain pointed a short distance behind them. It seemed as if the waves hit a wall and then broke.

Harry said in a low voice, "Give a wide berth to the southwest coast." It was what Vita had told him. She had warned Harry to give this part of the journey a wide berth, but it was lost on him. Harry had not relayed or even remembered that comment.

"What was that, Sir?" The captain hadn't been able to hear what he had said.

"Nothing," Harry replied, shaking his head. "What do we do now?"

The captain looked at the future king blankly. "We either wait, or try to get some oars into the water. We have some in the lower decks, but we don't have enough manpower to go far. We'd have to rest the men often until we get wind again, if we do. I cannot explain this at all, Sir."

Harry thought for a minute, "What if we go back and try to follow around where the damned sea changes?"

"Trying to turn this boat around with the few men we have will be difficult. We weren't manned for a voyage of manual rowing. I would prefer to move forward and try to catch a wind. But it's your call, Your Highness."

"You are the seasoned sailor. I will take your advice. Let's get a little momentum going." Harry turned again and looked at the rippling chop of the water in the distance. Before yesterday, he would never have thought this was something magical. Now he couldn't imagine it being anything but.

Chapter 15

When Jack woke up, it was still early evening, and he could hear the sentries walking around the camp. He was hungry and wanted something to eat. He was craving something fresh. His hunger had increased so much over the last two days; he couldn't explain it.

He quietly got off his cot and put on his trousers and boots, opened the flap of his tent, and looked around for the men keeping guard.

One of the men noticed him. "Good evening, Mr. Smark. Is everything ok?"

"Yes, just need to run to the woods to piss." Jack didn't have to piss, but he didn't need someone watching over him as he looked for something to eat.

"Be careful, Sir. It's pretty dark out tonight with the cloudy sky."

"Thanks. Carry on," Jack said as he walked into the woods a few yards away from the camp.

Once he reached the treeline, he looked back to make sure he wasn't still being watched.

The guards were all looking in the other direction. He darted off into the woods.

After a few minutes, he stopped and propped himself against a tree. His senses were getting sharper; he could feel when someone or something something was around. He could smell the life and energy of the animals as they got closer. He could sense it even from the soldiers he was with.

As he sat there, he started to feel that energy again. It was getting closer, coming from behind him, on the other side of the tree. It wasn't a large animal, but it was bigger than a rabbit.

He sat patiently, waiting as the animal start to come around the tree. Jack slowly stood up. As the creature rounded the tree, Jack jumped on it and tackled it to the ground. It was a baby forest deer. He sat on it as the poor fawn struggled under him.

Suddenly Jack's eyes started to glow bright orange. He reached down his hands and in one quick snap, he broke the deer's neck. Before the life could drain away, he took the front leg to his right and ripped it off, peeling the skin from the flesh down the deer's side. With his eyes still glowing, Jack crouched down and bit a large piece of still-living flesh off the deer and began eating.

∞ ∞ ∞

Jack woke up feeling like he barely slept. The captain and lieutenant were already out of the tent. He sat up groggily. The dream he had just been having felt so real, and was so disturbing; ripping apart a deer?

He went to put his head in his hands and suddenly jumped up out of the cot. He looked down at his hands in horror.

They were covered in dried blood.

He went over to where the captain kept his shaving bowl and mirror. There was blood all over his face, too.

Jack didn't know what the hell was going on. There was water in the bowl; he used it to rinse his hands and face. He took a towel and wiped it all off. Then he noticed his shirt was full of blood. He pulled it off and used the towel to wipe off the left-over blood on his neck.

He rolled up the shirt and towel and and hid them in his bag. Then he put on a clean shirt.

Jack sat back down on his cot and gripped the edge with his hands. He was confused and scared. He tried to remember what happened last night. Then the dream came shooting back. It wasn't a dream! Why would he do that to a deer – and more, why would he eat it raw? None of this made any sense.

He looked around for his pants to put them on, and then noticed he was still in his pants and boots from the night before.

Just then, the tent flap opened. It was Persy. He looked at Jack. "Good, you're up. You were snoring so loudly under your blanket this morning, I thought you were going to inhale it."

Jack looked at him blankly. "I didn't sleep well. Is there any coffee out there?"

"Sure is," Persy replied, "and some fresh morning pudding, or whatever the cooks call that stuff they feed us."

Jack could barely manage a chuckle. He stood up and the two walked over to the cook's tent, took bowls of food, and went to sit on a crate by the fire. One of the men brought Jack a cup of coffee.

Jack took a bite of what was in the bowl, but it made his stomach churn. After an awkward moment, he set the bowl on the ground in front of him. He started drinking the coffee; this is what he needed. The same soldier walked by again and Jack raised his cup for the man to fill it up for him.

"Not hungry?" Persy asked.

"Not this morning," replied Jack tersely.

"You didn't each much dinner last night either. It was good rabbit, too. Are you feeling all right?" Persy looked concerned. "You've been a bit off for the last two days, since you were sick after returning from getting the water."

Jack tried to brush it off. "Yes, I am fine. Just

getting used to living out in the wild, I guess. A good night's sleep will fix it all up." Jack wasn't sure if he was trying to convince Persy or himself. "I should be filling up the water jugs so we can be on our way on time."

He finished his coffee and took the bowl and cup to the cooks. Then he gathered up the jugs he filled every day for the men and made his way to the river.

When he was a few yards into the woods, he heard a commotion ahead. He paused, and then began walking slowly toward the rustling in the tall grass. Suddenly, three large scavenger birds flew out of the grass and knocked him flat on his back.

Jack lay there for a minute, catching his breath. Then he stood up and gathered the scattered jugs. He moved forward a few steps, cautiously – and then he saw the grotesque site where the birds had come from. It was the bloody carcass of a baby deer, the legs ripped off, eyes gouged out, half of its flesh eaten.

Now he knew for certain it wasn't a dream. He dropped to his knees, and whatever was in his stomach suddenly came up violently. His stomach heaved over and over. When he finally calmed down, he forced himself to look down at the deer. He was disgusted by the sight. But then, somewhere in his mind… it looked appetizing.

His stomach heaved again. He stood, still retching, and tried to shake off the feeling. He circled the carcass and told himself this was all just a mistake. This couldn't be happening. He decided he would forget about it. Jack picked up the water jugs and went to the river. He would avoid this site on his way back.

∞ ∞ ∞

Gevan woke up and could see out the wind that the sun wasn't fully risen yet. The previous day had been pretty uneventful, Strand had given him a tour of the castle and the grounds. They had shared dinner with some of the residents of the castle. Then Gevan had retired to the room they had given him in the northeast tower.

It was early, but Gevan hadn't slept well the previous night; he had not been able to stop thinking about Harry, Old Fraycia, his father, his mother and Lily. So much on the line, and he didn't even know what he was up against yet. How was he going to be ready in a year?

He looked around his room. The bed was across from the door with two tables on each side of it. There was a four-drawer dresser and a table with a water basin on the left side wall, and a window on the right, with a simple wooden desk and chair. It was a simple room, with bare furnishings and unadorned walls, but he had everything he would need.

Gevan reached over to the table on his right and picked up the book lying there. He stared at the cover. There was no writing, just a symbol of a what looked like a shining star in a dark country sky. Strand had given it to him the previous night; it was supposed to explain the basics of harnessing one's magical abilities.

Most magic revolved around spells – short incantations to make what the user willed to happen. The fireball he had summoned in Old Fraycia didn't use an incantation; it was a simpler, instinctive spell, just him envisioning what he wanted. According to Strand, such instinctive magic was a rare gift.

Gevan opened to book and began to read. He quickly became so absorbed in the text that he almost didn't hear the knock at the door. "Come in," he announced.

The door opened and Martin, the young librarian's assistant Gevan had met last night, breezed in. "Good morning, Master Gevan," He said briskly. "Breakfast will be served downstairs in an hour."

"Thank you. But please, just call me Gevan." He didn't like titles; it even made him uncomfortable when he was with Harry in Fraycia.

Martin replied, "Yes, Sir."

Gevan chuckled. "No Sir. No Master, or anything like that, please, Martin. Just Gevan."

Martin seemed to relax a bit. "Very well, Gevan."

"I will be down in a bit. Thank you for coming up." Gevan sat up and Martin left the room, closing the door behind him.

Gevan walked over to his water basin and poured some water from the large clay pitcher into the bowl. Then he bent down and put his hands in the cool water and splashed some on his face.

He opened his eyes – and he was standing in the middle of a forest.

In front of him someone was bent over what seemed to be a dead animal. He walked closer and could see it was a baby deer. But the figure was dark, and he couldn't make out any features.

He stepped closer and saw to his horror that the person was eating the deer while there was some life still left in it. Gevan felt sick to his stomach.

The figure suddenly jerked, and his head snapped around as if noticing Gevan was there. Then suddenly the figure's eyes exploded in a bright orange flare of light.

Gevan jumped back with his face dripping with water. He was back in his room. He grabbed the towel and wiped off his face. This wasn't a dream; it was a vision. It was the same figure he had seen in his dream standing next to him on the cliff. The figure felt familiar somehow, which made Gevan even more uneasy.

By the time he had come to his room last night, somebody had unpacked him. He looked through the drawers of the dresser to see where everything was. He pulled out a pair of socks, a clean shirt, and undergarments.

After getting dressed, he went down to the main floor, where the dining room was, toward the west end. He had some time before breakfast, so he wanted to stop by the library to see if there was a book on visions and dreams.

The library was empty. The soft white glow in the room seemed to come from nowhere. As he entered, the glowing light got brighter. Gevan thought to himself that he needed to learn this spell; it would save so much on candles and oil.

He wasn't sure where to even begin looking for a book that could help him. The walls were covered from floor to ceiling with shelves of books in all colors and sizes. He didn't even know how the library was organized.

"Can I help you, young sorcerer?" came a voice from behind him.

Gevan was a bit shocked; he had heard no sound of someone approaching. He turned and saw a thin, older man a few inches shorter than him. He had dark hair, graying at the temples, and dark blue eyes. He was wearing a simple tan robe, tied with a brown rope at the waist, and sandals.

"Aldred, you startled me." Gevan had met the librarian last night at dinner, but they had not had much time to talk.

Gevan was hesitant to continue, but after a moment he dived in. "I keep having these dreams, and the occasional vision when I am awake. I don't understand some of them. I don't know if they are just dreams, something from the past like I have with my father, or something else."

Aldred thought for a moment, then walked over to a book shelf across from the door, to the left of the window. He reached up a hand and a book floated down to him from the top shelf. It was a large book, very thick, with a dark brown leather cover cracking from age.

He walked over to the large reading table and set the book down. "Come over here."

Gevan walked over to stand next to him. "Will this help?"

The old librarian was intent on the pages he was flipping. "It depends on what you define as help. This book has many descriptions of dreams, from the basics of people believing when they dream about spiders it has some special meaning, to how visions happen while we are awake. I cannot guarantee you will find what you seek in here, but it is the most comprehensive book we have."

Finally he stopped flipping through the book and selected what appeared to be the start of a chapter or section. "I would start here." Aldred slid the book in front of Gevan. "I will have someone bring you breakfast here; I imagine you are going to be here a while."

Gevan looked up from the closely written pages in front of him. "Thank you!"

Aldred nodded. "I will let Strand know at

breakfast where you are." He turned and left, as quietly as he had appeared.

Gevan grabbed a chair and sat down, scanning the page Aldred had opened the book to. The page was titled "Visions of Loved Ones" He wasn't sure why Aldred had started him here; maybe because he had mentioned the dreams with his father.

Gevan read through breakfast and lunch. Strand had come to visit after breakfast, and he told the old mage about the disturbing vision he had had that morning. Strand knew this was a major concern for Gevan, and it was best to allow him to explore it and not push any training that day.

Through the reading, Gevan began to understand that some magicians could tap into the energy of their loved ones when they were in trouble or during highly emotional times. It could be controlled, to either focus on the person or to block them out.

It wasn't like reading their minds; it was more like they were calling out for help. If not controlled, they would know when anything happened, even if it was simply someone cutting their finger. Luckily, Gevan hadn't experienced a lot of these visions. But he couldn't help but wonder who he was connecting with then, if it was a loved one.

It was almost dinner when Gevan realized he hadn't had a break from reading all day. He needed some fresh air; he decided to take a walk outside.

∞ ∞ ∞

The *Serpent of the Sea* pulled into dock. The deck hands threw the ropes to the dock crew to help stabilize the boat. The crew began to tie up the sails and prepare for disembarking.

The captain left the helm and started barking orders to everyone, though most were seasoned and already knew their jobs when docking. Grange wanted to make sure everything was secure.

"Boy!" Grange called out to a deck hand nearby. "Go below and wake up Prince Harry. Let him know we have arrived."

"Aye, Captain." The boy ran down the stairs by the center mast. At the bottom he ran to the door at the end of the hall and knocked.

He heard the prince holler, "Come in."

He opened the door and bowed. "Your Highness, the captain wanted me to advise you we have arrived and are getting ready to disembark."

"Thanks, lad. Let him know I will be up shortly," replied Harry. With that the boy closed the door and went back up on deck.

Harry sat up in bed. He seemed to have had his best night's sleep in a while. He used the bathroom, then started to get dressed and join the crew on the deck.

His clothes were laid out on the bench at the end of his bed with his freshly polished boots. He pulled on his trousers and sat down on the bench to put on socks and his boots. He sat there for a minute; he seemed to be having a difficult time waking up.

After he finished getting dressed, he left his quarters and entered the dining area on the right. There was coffee and a sweet roll on the table. He grabbed the cup and sweet roll and went up on deck.

Captain Grange was waiting for him at the top of the stairs. "Good morning, Your Highness."

"Good morning, Captain. Seems we had a fairly good night." Harry hadn't felt any disturbance in the sea, which was probably why he had slept so well.

"Yes Sir, we did."

The plank was dropped, and the dock captain walked up to the top and greeted the prince and ship's captain. "Welcome home, Your Highness. Your brother sent a carriage for you; they are expecting you to join them for breakfast."

Standing at the railing, Harry gazed around at the kingdom he was soon to rule.

∞∞∞

Gevan had been on Bone Isle for a week now. He had read the entire book about dreams and visions but was no closer to knowing who he had been dreaming of; at least this week had been free of dreams and visions.

It was early still in the morning, and breakfast wouldn't be ready for an hour, so he went out for a short morning walk. The castle was five minutes from the cliffs and the sea between the island and the mainland. Over the past several days, Gevan had found peace sitting by the cliffs, gazing out over the water toward the mainland, barely more than a dusky green line on the horizon.

He reached the cliff and sat down on the rock he had come to relax on. A morning breeze came off the water, and he closed his eyes and listened to the waves crashing on the rocks below. It was all he could hear.

After a few peaceful moments, he opened his eyes and looked around. The cliff where he sat dropped off several dozens of feet to the rocks below. He estimated it was as tall as the castle towers, maybe more. He was never one to be scared of heights though, so occasionally he would look over the edge.

He heard something new, not the wind and not the waves. It was too steady and rhythmic.

Gevan stood and looked around but didn't see anything. The sound got louder.

Suddenly he saw a large winged creature in the sky, coming out of the bright morning sun, heading right for him. Gevan instinctively took a step back – and tripped over a rock. Before he could recover his footing, he felt himself falling backward off the cliff. He plummeted toward the waves below and the jagged rocks they crashed on to. His only focus was on the creature in the sky above him as he fell to certain death.

<h1 style="text-align:center">*Epilogue*</h1>

The king sat on his throne of black stone resting in the middle of a raised platform. It was in an open courtyard; the only wall was behind him. He was surrounded by various creatures of different forms. Some looked like their teeth could rip the heart out of a dragon, while others looked like house pets.

King Savnok was getting impatient waiting for Ta's return. "Where is the sentry?" His voice carried and echoed so all around him could hear. He had the head of a lion, but the body of a man, and he wore a long black cloak that draped around him. When standing, he was easily ten feet tall.

A small demon approached, all gray except for his bright red eyes the tip of his short tail, which also was red. He had hooves on his feet and hands with short claws.

"My King." The demon knelt. "Ta has not returned. We sent another scout but there was no sign of him."

Savnok stood and stepped down off the dais to stand in front of the small demon kneeling at his feet. In a deep commanding voice, he spoke to all those in his courtyard. "Our time is soon. We need to ensure our survival if we are to build a new world."

He threw open his cloak. Just like the rest of the demons, he was naked underneath. He lifted his left arm, which was scarred from being burned. When he moved, it was stiff and difficult to extend.

Curling his raised hand into a fist, the Demon King shouted, "We will not be beaten again! I will not accept failure." With that he looked down at the demon still kneeling before him. "You have failed me."

Savnok lifted his leg, and with his bare foot slowly squashed the little demon. A shrill of agony came from beneath his foot, until what sounded like the popping of a bubble from a child's gum. Deep red-black blood came from under the king's foot and between his toes.

The king pinned those around him with a burning glare. "Now send a scout to find a way through the wall of magic that confines us to this dark hole and scorched human land." He turned and returned to his throne.

After he sat down, he let out a loud roar that shook the wall behind him and the pillars surrounding the courtyard. "GO!"

All the demons stampeded in a panicked mob out of the courtyard, desperate to satisfy the Demon King's demand. All except one. A deep red demon with a human-shaped body approached the throne, confidently but cautiously. He had a head that looked mostly human, but with a single large horn sprouting from between his deep black eyes and curving back over his hairless head. His ears were pointed, and twice the size of a human's.

"My King," he said as he smoothly knelt, "I may have come up with a solution."

"What are you waiting for?" Savnok said in an irritated tone.

The demon looked up at his king. "We have discovered a new source of Marpa's energy."

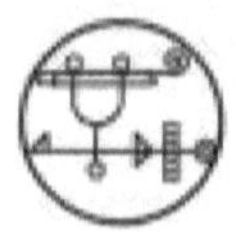